ZACHAEL T.J. PRESGROVE

The Tribes of Enthedrill

To the ones who are fighting against all oppression
and inequality...
This one's for you.

Contents

Foreword

I started off *The Kult of Salom'Sileyu* with a statement that I understood that not everyone shared my views and belief. I still stand by that. I will always make it a point to acknowledge that I am one person, and my views and beliefs are mine - just as yours are yours. But as I did with the first novel I wrote, I do now in making sure you're aware of what you're getting yourself into as you read this book. Most importantly, I urge you to respect those views, and if you can't, then it's okay to set the book down and walk away. It's simply not meant for you, and that's perfectly fine.

That being said, if you do decide that you want to give it a try and you've read my first novel, all I ask is that you respect the heart and intent poured into its pages. I write out of a love for humanity altogether. My hope is that my work might inspire the spark of change that can fix some of societies deepest problems. I hope to break the stereotypes passed down through the ages, and present heroes and villains of all races, all sexualities, and express some of life's deepest themes and questions through their lives and adventures.

I still stand by what I said; it's not always the strong, nordic man that's the hero. It's not always the emotionally stable that's the hero. It's not always the one who has their wits about them. It's not always the straight ones, the white ones, or the perfect ones. Sometimes, it's the hurt and heartbroken, the weak, the queer, the females, or the people of color that take part in saving the day. Sometimes it's the background characters that have a hand in helping the hero make it to the end, or saving them from destroying themselves in their emotional outbursts.

I hope this work of fiction helps you to see things a little differently. I hope that it helps us all appreciate our neighbors a little more, value money a little less, and seek to give more than to take. Most of all, I hope you all walk away from this story with a connection that helps you grow into the wonderful person you were always meant to be.

Readers, may I present for your literary enjoyment, the sequel to the Kult of Salom'Sileyu;

The Tribes of Enthedrill

Acknowledgement

As I stated before, there are many friends and family that helped get me to this point - too many to name in this section - but primarily, I want all those who helped to inspire and shape this world of mine that know that this is the product of the love and labor they poured into me. Be as proud of it as I am.

Thank you to my God, my friends, and my family that all supported me through every step of the way to getting to this point. I wouldn't have gotten here without you

Literary by Zachael T.J. Presgrove

The Salom'Sileyu Trilogy
The Kult of Salom'Sileyu
The Tribes of Enthedrill

I

Episode 1

Murder

Chapter 1

What an interesting thought that was...

To write down in a letcher for my lost child...

"Did you know you were the child of royalty while you were still alive?"

Rain poured in sheets from the slate-colored storm clouds above, covering the elevated forest-city in a glistening wet that reflected the night lamps that shared their light. It was a storm of sorrow: no lightning or thunder. It was the storm of a grieving mother and an angry father. And there he stood on his balcony of the palace built into the tree, overlooking the vast capital city of Centerton, Songriveii. His deep, maroon locks were tied into a bun behind his head, soaked by the rain as his golden eyes looked out past the treetops of the forest his city was built into. The horizon was obscured by darkness, just as his heart was with burning rage. His clenched fists tightened, and the rain seemed to fall harder.

He sighed and turned towards his bed chambers, where his magenta-haired wife sat on their bed with a somber look on her face. They were the Sovereign and Sovereignness of Songriveii, the ruling family of all the noble houses of their blessed country, and the purest of pure-bred blood elves – a term he learned to embrace, despite the disgusted tone other nations took when they gave it to him. They were Amadeus and Numira Renn.

She looked up at him with sorrowful blue eyes, and forced a smile as best as she could. This day, so long ago, they lost their child, Tsana Renn. Vanished without a trace, they presumed the infant dead, and have given up hope so long ago. But two things have remained since that black day...

...A mother's pain...

...And a father's wrath.

He knew what had happened deep in his heart; Emperor Gorvon Komin of Enthedrill had his child kidnapped and assassinated. The Emperor has longed to expand his borders, and he often tested the patience of the Sovereignty by nearing ever closer with airships and submarines. Not too long after Tsana's death, though, Amadeus accused the Emperor, and when the Emperor sent troops to occupy the port towns of his country, he launched an attack that erupted into the war the Sovereignty and the Empire fight to this very day.

"Amadeus," Numira cooed, pulling him from his thoughts. "Come and hold me, please."

He silently obeyed, taking a seat on their bed beside her and wrapping her in his arms. "Why have the gods blessed us with a son, but took our daughter away from us?" She began to cry. He held her tighter.

"Numira," he said softly, pulling her chin up and looking into her eyes, "none of the divine ones were involved in this – you know that... This was the work of a wretched man... One whose lands the gods of the Korists plague. He is a man who cannot take responsibility for his actions. The gods of Songriveii laugh at the gods of the Enthedrill, and will give us the vengeance we seek," he promised. Numira began to cry softly.

"I don't want vengeance... I want Tsana... She was so tender... So innocent... That *bastard* took her from us! I curse his gods! I curse his empire! May our blood be the end of him!" She shouted. The walls, floor, and ceiling rippled from the sound of her voice, as if they were the surface of a pond being disturbed by a lowly pebble. He marveled; she

5

was a divine logician – once a common people, and now a rare occurance. He knew she wasn't alone, either. He'd heard tales of the logician named Rhaja who gave her life fighting the Empire from within. His own son, Kudaj, began to show signs of the logicians at a very young age, and has honed them ever since. Even the ruling house of Easton have grown into their own abilities as well.

Amadeus felt terrified, awestruck, and entirely infatuated with his wife as she released her power. He held the back of her neck and caressed her, and she held his hand. "He will meet his end, Numira... And it will be as bitter as he deserves it to be," he reassured her. "I promise you..."

Chapter 2

Current day...

2 years after the events of the catastrophe of Vör....

"Once, there was a vast emptiness," the congregant master said as he opened his sacred scriptures. "Then, Rök shattered his divine soul, and matter exploded forth into the emptiness. Thus, the universe was created. This is a story we all know and love, fellow Korists."

Kamille shifted in the pew uncomfortably beside Ayela. It wasn't because the seat was uncomfortable, nor was it anything they were wearing – they dressed quite casually, in fact. It was more because Kamille hated religion. She hated the thought of an organization controlling and manipulating people through the thin veil of spirituality.

Ayela believed differently, though. She mostly adhered to the tenants of Korism. She believed in its statutes, that all reman should be treated as equals and that they should only immerse into Korism if their hearts don't hold any conflict over it. Kamille didn't come over religion, though, and Ayela didn't force her to come; she got a lead from the mysterious leader of their illusive guild, *the Darklings.* There was a member of this congregation leadership that belonged to *them...* The *Kult...*

It was personal for Ayela. Just two years ago, the love of her life was stolen from her because of the horrible goals of the deep-state order that named themselves the Kult of Salom'Sileyu. She shuddered as she remembered everything that happened. Any time she heard of a Kult member in any place of leadership, she made it a personal mission to take them down, albeit as inconspicuously as possible. Kamille understood that, and apparently, so did their hidden leader, *Ruat.*

"And we all know what happens next... N'Adan and his wife, Kudoru – the first remans – sought the fruit of the Great Tree of Red for eternal life. Against the will of Rök, they took and ate, and were greated by the Towlål, who gave them the knowledge of sadness, wrath, and warpedness... Because of the actions of our first ancestors, we as a species, fell into darkness, and death was introduced. Our immortality was stripped from us, and our invincibility was erased. With a sorrowful heart, Rök threw them to Thaerv, and wrapped them in mortal flesh so that our immortal souls would experience the death of animals, and those Tormentors were given dominion over the universe they polluted," the preacher preached, Kamille rolled her eyes and slouched a little more.

"You actually believe this, Ayela?" She whispered.

Ayela smirked. "If you'd read the Alldweii a little more intently, you might find that it makes more sense than you think."

Kamille rolled her eyes. "No thanks. I think I'll pass. The idea of divine logicians is crazy enough for me. The fact that extra-dimensional beings exist is more than enough, with the Aethril attacks and all," she retorted.

Ayela hadn't noticed the long pause the preacher gave, but before she could respond, he began to cough uncontrollably. Several congregants gasped, and the girls leapt from their seats as he doubled over. Panicked, Ayela ran over to him and caught him before he fell to the ground. Though she and Kamille had only been living in Ih'Dejj for half a year, she'd grown quite fond of the Congregation Master. He was the most accepting, understanding, and compassionate man she'd ever met. Even Kamille had grown to like him, which was hard for her considering her negative disposition to ivory

9

elves.

"Master Gillain?" Ayela panicked. "I'm here, Master Gillain. Keep breathing. Stay with me."

Kamille was trying to keep the peace with the other congregants, urging them to remain seated and calm while she and a few others got a hold of medical professionals. "Ayela," Gillain wheezed.

"I'm here," she reassured through teary eyes.

"You are a light in this world... You... You're the most unique reman that has ever been born... Rök has whispoered to my inclining ear that you have a touch of destiny... And your path... Not even time... T-time... Can t-touch..." He said between coughs as he drew his final breath.

"NO!" Ayela shouted. Others began to wail at the loss of their beloved preacher. "Get up! Breath! You can't give up!" She cried as she tried to jostle him back to consciousness. "GET UP!" She screamed.

"Ayela," Kamille cooed, slowly making her way over. "He's dead, Ayela..."

Then, Ayela noticed a particular smell, and watched in horror as a sage-colored ooze slowly flowed from his nostrils. She recognized it immediately from one of the documents she and Kamille leaked to the public: a government funded program that explored different kinds of biological weapons to use in assassination attempts.

"Kamille," she said in a hushed tone. Her heart

started to burn with anger. "Do you see this?" She asked as she pointed to it. Kamille immediately knelt down and sniffed the air around the body.

"It's the Irffil Pathogen!" She exclaimed, standing to her feet.

"He was assassinated?!" Someone from the congregation said in a worried tone.

"It's just like the darklings said in their online posts!"

"The government is targeting religious leaders?!"

Then, a tall, handsome ivory elf with slicked blonde hair and beady green eyes stood to his feet. "Ayela!" Kamille whispered in a panicked tone. "It's him! It's the cultist!"

"Hear me, congregation!" He shouted, demanding their attention. "The empire has failed us! They seek to snuff out the light of Korism! This assassination on our beloved master is all the proof we need!"

Ayela stood to her feet, tapping into her reservoirs of divine logic for use at any moment. "Don't, Ayela. Not here. You know your abilities are illegal in this country," Kamille whispered, urging her to back down. Ayela reluctantly obeyed. Her heart was distraught, angry, and confused simultaneously. Every instinct told her to attack – to incapacitate and turn him in. She knew, though, that he would suffer no harm. He would be let go. And then the news of her survival would be public, and the chaos of the empire knowing that divine logicians were still around would lead to too much death.

"What are we going to do?!" One of the congregants panicked.

The cultist cleared his throat. "We're going to rise up! We're going to fight back!"

"No!" Ayela protested. "It's not right. That's *exactly* what they want."

"And what if we stay still and do nothing, *blood elf*? We'll lay down and die? I say fight! There's a government representative here, isn't there?"

With horror, she watched as the congregation turned to glare at the police officer that regularly attended with them. Kamille grabbed her hand; they could both *feel* what was about to happen. She didn't want to believe it. She wished she could focus more on the cultist's degenerate insult rather than the elevated primal instinct she could sense from the other elves in the chapel with them, but she knew it would have been a false hope. Something had overtaken them – something that both she and Kamille found themselves immune to.

"Stop!" She pleaded. "Don't do this! What's gotten into all of you?! Mrs. Tellasta, remember telling me after congregation three weeks ago how you just couldn't understand the wars going on!?"

Her pleas were to no avail, though. A dark, twisted magic had fallen over them, exerted from the dark logic that the cultist influenced with. The Kult of Salom'Sileyu was planning something big, and she could *see* Tallie's fingerprints all over it.

Without saying a word, the rest of the congregants leapt at the officer and dragged him to the stage of the chapel while the cultist pulled out his phone to record. She and Kamille quickly dashed off the stage, eagerly escaping the phone's camera, but Ayela saw a wicked grin creep across his face as he watched. He was *pleased* with their demented state of mind. He bore the same nasty energy that Tallie did.

The officer screamed, and she watched in terror as some of the stronger, more brutish men pulled out knives and began to cut into his limbs. She clasped her hands over her mouth as the crimson blood and the stomach-churning gore splattered on the bloodthirsty congregants, and before Kamille dragged her out, she saw them rip his head off with their bare hands.

Ayela shrieked, and she couldn't hear anything else around her. It was something out of a nightmare, and she hoped deep in her gut that she would wake from it. Kamille's persistence in their departure returned her to reality, and she saw the pedestrians that had stopped to gawk in confusion.

She felt their gazes. It was as if she were standing there stark naked. The crimson-haired elf hadn't noticed that she was crying as a tear fell from her cheek, and she quickly wiped her face as her dark elf friend led her away from the chapel.

"Someone call the police!" Kamille ordered. "One of their own was murdered in that chapel!"

Most stood there in disbelief, leaving only the gentle breeze of the sunny day and the quiet hum of some of the cars as they passed by fill the void of sound. "NOW!" She barked. It was obvious that they couldn't call the cops: their involvement with the darklings and the incoming questioning of investigators put them at too much risk. They needed a friend. They needed *Karinth*.

To her relief, one of the men made the call, and they took off running in the distance. They had a bigger case at hand than they previously anticipated, and a longer journey before finally finding rest. Ayela's heart sank as they turned a corner and vanished out of sight. Why target the Korists? Why target such a peaceful people?

...What was the Kult planning?

Chapter 3

They sat on Kamille's couch as she made phone calls. Ayela rested her elbows on her knees and let her thoughts wander. She tried to find a reason that would justify framing them, and the only thing that came to mind was the ancient hidden war between the Towlålites and the Uri'Kai, but she wasn't so sure that it was the culprit. This was a tactic... This was a *set up*. Organizations don't make moves like this unless they were intent on justifying something much bigger than a secretive conflict.

She mindlessly turned on the TV and changed the channel to the news, and watched as the events from earlier that day filled the background of the reporter's backdrop. She seemed to have changed the channel just in time, too, as the scrawling text revealed that the emperor had a statement he was preparing to release to the public. "Wow. National television already. This was a pretty big deal," Kamille spat. She had no love for cops, that was certain. It didn't mean that she wanted to watch one killed so brutally, though. And that particular officer had a good relationship with the dark elf that she couldn't say she had with any other. "Guess I shoulda seen that one coming."

"It's the cops. Of course they'll make a big deal," Ayela chimed in sarcastically.

Their attention was stolen, however, as the emperor's face appeared on the screen. "It's starting," Ayela hushed, waving Kamille over to the couch. \

The dark-haired, crimson-eyed ivory elf cleared his throat before he began to speak. "A tragedy has struck this day. Across the nation, in all major holds, attacks were made in the halls of Korist chapels against local police officers and religious Congregant Masters. An equal fifty officers and fifty masters were brutally killed, as many of you have seen on your local channels at this point." The girls looked at each other, shook at the revelation that theirs wasn't the only chapel that experienced this horrific tragedy. "It's for the safety of this nation's fine men and women in uniform, as well as the safety of Korists everywhere that I am outlawing the public worship and practice of the Korist religion, effective immediately. Chapels will be reclaimed by Hold-Governments, and those congregants who attended will be generously compensated. Any Alldweii's being sold in book stores are to be discontinued and discarded, and any public possession will be fully punishable according to the law. Keep your texts indoors. Keep your worship hidden. Whoever is behind these attacks; they will be sought out to the fullest extent, and they will be sentenced to a traitor's death. Only then will we have peace."

"What?!" Ayela said with an exacerbated tone. "Korism is *outlawed?!* He can't do that!" She yelled. Kamille gently caressed her back as she sank her face into her hands and let out a bitter wail.

"As for the extremists responsible for this uprising; you have yourselves to blame for the outlawing of your faith. You hid under the banner of a peaceful people, and chose to shock its members with acts of brutal, barbaric violence. Those who got away will not be hidden for long. Those who claimed that the return of the tyrannical divine logicians was at hand... Your words will be silenced, and the nightmares you wreak on my peaceful people will be at an end," the emperor finished. His image disappeared from the screen, but before the anchor could continue her thoughts, loud cries and angry screams filled the air outside. Kamille and Ayela rushed to the window to see people rushing out into the streets to form a riot. Within seconds, things were being thrown into windows, cars were being smashed in my bats and rods, and people started to raise their fists at the police who frantically tried to keep the peace.

"What the *Hell* is going on?!" Kamille stammered, confused at the sudden chaos.

"We have to do something," Ayela urged.

"No. There's nothing we can do."

"You and I both know that's bullshit, Kamille!"

Gently, she placed her hands on Ayela's shoulders. "On the contrary, love, *you* know what I'm saying is true. What are you going to do? Use your powers, signal the return of the Uri'Kai, and make this situation even more dangerous for those civilians? You know they won't hesitate to destroy homes and gun people down-"

As she spoke, the sounds of machine-guns ripped through the rest of the noise outside, and panicked screams erupted louder than the angry shouts. Ayela's heart sank. "What are we going to do?" She pleaded.

"We need to get out of this city. I've arranged for us to stay in Shamol where Thillan is. Asher will meet us there, too. Together with them, we'll figure out a plan and discover the truth behind all this," Kamille explained. Ayela took a deep breath and tucked the loose strands of her crimson hair behind her pointed ear, and her violet eyes drifted to the window as she stared at the outside world. So much escalated in a single day. So much had gone so wrong, she didn't even know how to mentally organize the events that transpired.

"How many days?" She asked. She couldn't think clearly, she was so distraught.

"Well, we have to make it to the path on Kör's cliff. Asher's arranged for another darkling cell to leave a vehicle for us to take. So, it's going to be three days on foot. The wilds up here aren't as dangerous in the mainland. Hell, there's even motels at the waypoints along the freeways – which is what we'll be heading towards. After that, it's a five-day drive. We'll stop at a few towns along the way."

Ayela took a deep breath and stood to her feet. They were going to be fine. She had to believe it. She shuddered at her last venture in the wilds of Enthedrill, when a giant creature tried to eat her after she'd wandered from the destruction of Sümol... She shuddered at the thought of it happening again.

"Alright," she sighed as Kamille slung a backpack over her shoulder. She pulled a pistol out from under the cushion and handed it to Ayela. "What's this for?"

"Just because we don't kill doesn't mean we can't incapacitate. If we're attacked, take out their knees or something. Avoid anything vital."

She took a deep breath. *So, the darklings aren't above guns and rifles... I guess in some circumstances, it makes sense.* She justified in her thoughts. She threw a white hoodie on and slung a backpack over her shoulder as well, and they took one last look at the apartment and sighed.

Despite her wishes, she knew things were going to get much, much harder...

Chapter 4

The next few days of theirs were spent in the wilds. On the night of the third day, though, Ayela could see the motel sign peering over the tops of the trees along the roads. It was a relieving sight. She didn't particularly like sleeping in the woods with nothing more than a hood to keep small insects and sticks out of her hair, but they made it work. Kamille had packed snacks for them to munch on along the way so, at the very least, they wouldn't starve. To the dancer, every little bit counted. She exhaled in relief that the motel was just ahead, which meant warmth for them, good sleep, and cleaning off all the dirt and grime they accumulated.

Small talk filled their time when they weren't wary of their surroundings, and she enjoyed it. Kamille had become her closest friend over the last two years. She was there when Ayela was able to properly grieve over Rhaja, not to mention that she helped her regain control over her emotions when she found out who killed her late lover. She was even her introduction into the darklings. Most importantly, though, she and Karinth helped Ayela settle into a semi-regular life.

"I'm ready for a soft bed," Kamille sighed as she stretched her arms. The grassy ground with roots and branches certainly didn't make for a good night's sleep.

Ayela snickered. "Or a shower," she added. "A shower, and perhaps a nice meal. You think Asher arranged that for us as well?"

"Most likely. He's a cold bastard, but he's not heartless."

"One could hope. How many times have you met Asher?"

"At least twice," Kamille revealed. "He's the only sort of leadership that's been appointed to the darklings besides Ruat. He meets with all the other cells across the country and relays information. We've done work with the branches in Metralonia and Ifnir to expose several corrupt politicians. The ones bribed their policemen to target any elf of color?"

"I remember seeing that on the news!" Ayela exclaimed.

"Yeah, that was us. We've leaked a few important pieces to the public. Our actions have done some decent work exposing the corruption in our government. Their influence on the public is definitely weakened, but it's not enough. We need something big. Finding out what's going on behind these attacks on congregations will be a crippling blow to the empire. This wreaks of conspiracy like the modern world has never seen."

"...I have a feeling that it's even bigger than that..." Ayela said as she looked up at the stary night sky. She said a silent prayer in her heart, hoping for some relief along the way of a seemingly perilous journey. She knew within the depths of her consciousness that there was something greater than nations and politics going on. The Kult was a doorway into a greater war going on behind the scenes that everyone else was blind to. A cosmic war of ancient gods and the warriors they called upon.

"Let's keep our minds from going there. The last thing we need to do is despair," Kamille said, pulling her back to reality. "We're here."

Ayela looked up and noticed the light peering through the trees, and finally saw the break in the wall of forest to make way for a large, empty parking lot save for a couple older cars. At the rear, stretching nearly to the road on the left, were all the motel rooms built side-by-side. Dim lights on the inside and stained walls, it had the appearance of an old stay-in that had certainly seen better days. The dark night with ominously tall trees made it seem like it wasn't safe, but she knew that the bright lights illuminating the dreary setting were engineered to keep the dangerous creatures of the Wilds at bay. Even the ones atop the cliffs had been known to venture onto the roads and into reman settlements sometimes...

...As long as the *bigger* ones stayed deep in the forests they dwelt.

A bell rang from above the door to the check-in office as then entered, filling the near-silence with obnoxious clanging that pierced their ears. A man sat behind the desk reading an old-style print newspaper, cliché in every manner of his appearance. He wore a yellow and red button-down flannel with stained jeans and worn boots. The sleeves were rolled up to reveal arms covered in dark hair, and his pointed ears drooped from his old age, and the depression he likely carried with him.

"How many nights," he said plainly.

Kamille cleared her throat and waited for him to lower his paper.

"How many damn nights?" He spat, angrily tossing the paper aside. Only after he saw him did his expression change from frustration to anxiety. "Shit- Sorry, ladies! They told me you'd be coming.

Your room is number four, and you're cleared for as many nights as you need. There's some things left there for you by your contact, and here's a key to that six-wheel drive sitting out front, by the room."

They followed his finger as he pointed out the window at an older car that sat all by its lonesome in front of a red-curtained window. The only thing that looked kept on it were the six shiny tires on its wheels – three on either side. Most cars that people drove through the wilds were required by law to have the tires and headlights up to date, lest they have an issue on the road and are subject to the horrors in the trees.

Kamille sighed. "At least it runs... I assume..." She said.

"Oh, and your contact told me to give you a message; *Stick to the shadows, you huddled foes, and in the shadows, your secrets're known,*" The clerk added. They smiled awkwardly at him as they took the keys to the room and car, and quickly left. Ayela felt like she'd seen enough stained yellow from that office to make her sick.

The room wasn't much better, but it was clear their contact did what they could to accommodate them with whatever they needed. The room smelled clean, the walls looked as though they were scrubbed, and the furniture at least had the appearance that it was kept up. Of course, Ayela would have preferred if they'd just came and picked them up on the side of the road, but they were the closest cell to them that could reach them in time, and they had their own objectives they had to complete in the town they were located in. She understood why, at the very least.

On the bed were two duffle bags that looked as though they were packed to burst. "Plenty of gear to get us through with our objective, yeah?" Kamille remarked, giddily rushing over to them. Ayela closed the door and sighed in relief.

"I'm just glad to have some kind of bed and shower," She said, leaning against the door.

Kamille wasted no time opening her bag and pulling out the items. Among the clothing, ration packs, money, and boots, there was also a rifle folded up at the bottom. Ayela felt her skin go numb at the sight, but she kept from showing it on her face. *There's a reason for it,* she thought to herself. *We aren't trying to kill anyone... Right?*

"You likely have the same things in your bag," Kamille said, setting the rifle down with the same apprehension in her movements that Ayela felt in her heart. "Right, let's settle in for the night. There's a reason Asher sent us all this gear, so we better trust his educated opinion."

Ayela raised an eyebrow as her friend made her way to the bathroom. After everything that happened in Vör, she analyzed everything she saw and heard like it was second nature, looking for hidden messages in everything. She knew she could trust Kamille, but she couldn't help but feel as though there was something she wasn't being told. Given the nature of the darklings, she wasn't entirely surprised – if one of them were captured, secrets could be shared that would do more than compromise their little mobile cell... But for any of their plan to work, she needed to trust and be trusted. As she set her duffle bag off to the side, she couldn't help but wonder...

...What are you hiding, Kamille? What did Asher tell you...

II

Episode 2

Sanctuaries

Chapter 5

Soldiers marched through the thick Songrivan forests, dressed from head-to-toe in crimson armor with golden trimming – the banner colors of the Songrivan national military. Their destination? Another port town ravaged by Enthedrillan invaders. This war had gone on too long. Too many Songrivan lives were lost at the hands of these conquerors, these invaders that sought what wasn't theirs.

Much too many lives.

But this day would be different. While the buildings were destroyed, homes were reduced to rubble, and walls were built to fortify the town into an enemy base, its citizens still lived on. They were forced into slave-labor, reduced to sub-elves under fascist control of the mighty empire. But in Kudaj's mind, they were a tyranny he was destined to take part in stopping.

His helmet disassembled and packed itself away into his armor, granting him full view of his troops with his own violet eyes. His jet-black locks were slicked back, and his face was patched with stubble. He hadn't shaved in quite some time. Around him were his scarlet warriors, dressed for combat against an enemy that was unfamiliar with their enchanted woods. At their hips were standard-issue swords, and held across their chest were their rifles. They carried everything they needed on their backs, and with each stride they carried the pride of the Sovereignty. He couldn't have been more proud to stand alongside such vicious warriors. And he too would aid them.

Him...

Kudaj...

The son of the Sovereign, marching into battle with two Korokian blades at his hips, and a lifetime of honing his potent divine logic. The empire wouldn't know what hit them. It would take all of the empire's navy and army to put him down. He had the power to back his confidence. His ego was not out of place.

Then, the smell of heated metal and burning wood filled his nose. *We're close enough*, he thought to himself. "Ready, men!" He barked. The soldiers lifted their rifles in unison and halted in their position. At the ready stood a battalion of nearly five thousand soldiers anticipating the rush of violent adrenaline. Their senses were all heightened, and their victory was already so close, they could taste it. They would push the enemy back, and Kudaj would taste the first droppings of revenge for their theft of his dear sister's life...

"CHARGE!!!" He screamed with ferocious volume. The men rushed passed him with those in the front activating their holoshields. It would be like no other charge that was ever led before this moment. He'd studied under the finest of Songriveii's tacticians, and now that his father had unleashed him with the full fury of the Sovereignty upon their invaders, he would turn the tide of this war – he was *certain* of it.

Finally, he drew his seemingly dull swords from their scabbards, and with a small flex of divine logic – so slight that it took no effort – violet beams of energy traced the edges of the bleached blades. His Korokian blades were activated, and the full might of the ancient Yglsora would be unleashed upon those that defied him.

Then he dashed forward with his men. Blades and shields alit, they were a picture of terror for the empire. It was evident, too; many of their soldiers panicked as they scrambled about atop the gates of their erected walls, rushing and clambering to get weapons and defend themselves. Kudaj's soldiers wore armor that enhanced their movement, though, and they were nearly upon them when the empire opened fire. Many of the bullets disintegrated upon contact with the shields, but some of them went through and ricoched off their armor. Only a few fell upon the initial assault.

When they arrived at the gate, Kudaj reached out with his hands and drew upon his reserves of magical ability. He then tore an opening through their gates with telekinetic prowess. His soldiers poured through the wound, and he performed a twirling leap. When he landed, he slammed his hand onto the ground and sent a rolling wave through the earth beneath, as if it were the surface of the ocean that reached to the horizon past the fort. When the wave reached the encampment, it burst forth from and sent imperial soldiers flying through the air. His Songrivan warriors knew better than to proceed forward when an attack like that was approaching, and Kudaj made sure that it didn't affect them in any way aside from the strange visuals it produced. They remembered the battle plan he'd gone over with them before departing on their campaign.

Seeing the success of their attack, he smirked and took a deep breath. There was shouting and gunfire filling his eardrums, but he tuned it all out in a moment of intense focus. He was the revival of the Yglsora, and they would fear him. With an exhale, he roiled all tension and anxiety, and was hyper aware of every sensation gliding across his body; from the sweat that dampened the cloth underneath his armor, to the cool breeze offered by the gods of the skies as they watched over his battle.

Then he gripped his swords tightly – they'd never left his hands even as he sent the wave through the ground – and let out his battle cry as he charged forward with bravado and terrifying rage. The empire would recognize his name on that day.

The first soldier was there, and he was upon him in an instant; driving the glowing blades of his swords effortlessly into the enemy's chest. The life quickly faded from his eyes, and Kudaj ripped his weapons from the carcass before rehearsing his most favored maneuvers from his training. Enemies fell before him as he effortlessly cut, stabbed, and swung at everyone that wasn't a conquered citizen or Songrivan warrior.

As his emotions heightened, he unleashed his magical prowess, and to any other ordinary person it would have looked as though he'd just appeared out of thin air in front of his next target. His movements were blindingly fast, but not fast enough. Bullets certainly hit his armor, but after one pierced through the joint at his knee, it sank deep into his flesh and bone and incapacitated him for a brief moment. He fell onto his good knee and breathed as the initial flashes of heated, searing pain passed, then he stood to his feet once more.

Every movement was filled with unimaginable pain. Every step he took, every swing at an Enthedrillan soldier, every pivot and turn – everything was filled with a memory of pain like he hadn't experienced. His resolve, though... His resolve was mighty. He absolutely and utterly refused to submit to his wound. The smell of gun smoke and rotting flesh was enough to churn the guts of any average reman that day, but he ignored it as he set his sights on his final target.

Suddenly, the sounds of metal clanging and gunfire became dull, and his body went numb from furiously pumping adrenaline. Emerging from the flame-engulfed tents and encampments was the commander of this occupying force; Commander Chuzok, the dark warrior of Enthedrill's navy.

There he stood as Kudaj's equal, dressed in his nation's military orange and slate colors painted on his armor. Like the son of the Sovereign, he wore two swords resting in scabbards at his hips, and his helmet was removed to reveal sandy-blonde hair tied into a tight bun behind his head, and a dark, braided beard draping from his chin. Bullets would fly in his direction, but in a similar fashin to when they would zip around Kudaj's head, they would change direction and pass him by if they were directed at Chuzok's...

He recognized the presence of another divine logician like himself...

But this one...

This one was different somehow.

The time for hesitation had passed, though. Now was the time for action, and if the empire had gotten their hands on a divine logician like himself, it was imperative that he put an end to the power within their grasp. He clenched his swords tighter, and roared with ferocity as his foe drew black blades like his own, edges lit with cyan beams. Then, as they drew within proximity, they raised their swords and swung with might, and their blades clashed with the loudest of an explosive sound, one that forced all others around them dropped their weapons and clenched their ears. All attention was now on them, and they would witness a modern fight between ancient orders...

...The Yglsora and the Towlålites.

Chapter 6

"War rages on both coasts, with away forces contin-uing to hold down the shores of Songriveii, and our own armies making sure to defend our coasts as well. Spending has increased by tens of millions of sigil just to keep up with the cost of maintaining arial naval ships and sea ships. The economy is on the brink of collapse, as more small business in all twelve holds and in several surrounding towns close their doors. Yet, despite this, mega chains like Illie's Supermart, Castora's, and Golem – three of the biggest corporate chains in the country – raked in more than three-point-six trillion sigil in last year's profits alone. More later when we return, I'm Helonica Mayim, channel seven news-"

"Bloody bastards," barked Thillan, a tall dark elf with short, braided hair and piercings lining his left ear. His voice was powerful, and his cockney accent was thick. His eyes were a deep ebony color, and his frame was cut and lean. He looked like he could outrun a fleet of military trucks – or punch his way through them. He wore a loose and baggy black tank top, harem pants held up by their in-built waist strings tied in a knot, and stylish sneakers to match. His right arm was covered in intricate tattoos that reached over his shoulder and onto his chest.

Sitting beside him was Asher. About as tall as Thillan, and just as uniquely styled. He was well-kept. His black hair was slicked back, and his facial hair was trimmed neatly. He was as fit as his friend, but he wasn't covered in ink – not that anyone would be able to tell. He wore a sage Henley with the top two buttons undone, which loosely draped down the waist of his black jeans. He wore dress shoes, and a nice watch on his wrist. He carried himself with beaming confidence, and presented an aura of mystery, allure and class.

"That they are, Thillan," Asher said, his voice smooth and velvet. "That's why these recent developments are so important. Your girlfriend and the new one should be here tomorrow. In the meantime, there's another job we have to take."

Thillan sighed. "Time to rough up a spook." He stood, cracked his neck, and grabbed the pair of knuckles Asher held out for him.

Their mission was simple, violent, and if all went right, everyone would walk home with no broken bones. There was someone who held information on one of the greatest vaults of imperial data, rumored to have been stored in D'Vnora since the dawn of the internet age, but they were only rumors... Until Asher had caught wind of an Enthedrillan official spotted walking out of an obscure, supposedly abandoned building. That same official was spending some R&R in Shamol, and it was perfect timing considering the massacres in the congregations across the country.

"We're only trying to extract information from him. If there's any sign of military support – not that the empire would dare try to break one of their oldest statutes – we're out," Asher explained, handing him a facemask and a wraparound voice changer.

"Don't need to tell me twice. I've got the rendezvous. If I have to, I'll call Kamille and have them meet us in Livvyton rather than here."

"Good. Let's get a move on."

Only a few blocks away, they slipped behind apartment buildings and stuck to the alleyways where there wasn't a soul in sight. It was one of the beauties of having someone like Thillan, who regularly frequented the small town with his girlfriend when they weren't off with their independent darkling cells, ravaging the empire's infrastructure with prejudice. They both slipped on black hoodies as per their plan, and Thillan couldn't have been more grateful that the season was the brisk cool of autumn.

Pulling him from his thoughts, Asher stopped at the corner of the building across from their destination. Satisfied that the coast was clear, they scurried across towards a small bar frequented by the town's locals. Many of the ones who came were sympathizers to the darklings, so when they saw someone new, there was a hesitation to make them feel welcome.

That day, their target was *anything* but welcome.

Asher slipped into the bar swiftly and gracefully, and Thillan wasn't far behind. The smell of stale cigarettes and potent alcohol wafted across his nose, and his mouth began to water for a strong whiskey. *Perhaps we can hit up one of the other bars near the apartment,* he thought to himself. He and Asher were close friends, and they often went out for a drink before and after a big mission. Even though this seemed small, the reward for the information they could get out of this op was *huge*.

His silver-tongued friend wasted no time between entering, spotting their target, and leading Thillan over to him. They slipped their arms through his and lifted him in such a way that any attempt to resist would hurt. Despite the protests, his grunts of pain and panicked begging were the only sounds that could be heard above the soft music and the clamoring of a knocked-over chair. Everyone turned their heads and let the two do what they were going to do. So they dragged him into the back while he shrieked like a frightened child.

Thillan kicked the door open, and the one after that. When they entered the manager's office, they sat him down in one of the metal folding chairs, and started hitting him over and over in the face until blood started to drip from his mouth and nose. One of his eyes was already swollen by the time they were done with him, and the tears readily streamed down his cheeks.

"What did I do to you guys?! Why are you doing this?! Please let me go!!" He screamed. His blonde hair was already a sweaty mess, and his hyperventilating echoed in the small office.

"You have access to the data-vaults in D'Vnora. We need that access," Asher demanded. His voice was obscured by the changer he wore.

"W-What?! You don't understand! None of you do! I know *exactly* who you are, darklings! You think you're just going to waltz into the vault like you own the place?!"

"Good. You confirmed its existence. Now tell us how to get in."

The official smirked after he coughed up blood. "You think it'll be that easy? Even if I tell you, you don't think they've planned every possible break in for the *most secure data vault* in the entire *country*? What, you think you can just fabricate ID's and walk through the front door? They have DNA analysis on every citizen of this country. They have facial recognition software, and they have... Officials... Operatives... Off-the-books types. There are no official records of their existence. You have absolutely *no chance* of breaking in-"

Thillan didn't let him get another word in before knocking him out. "Asher, this is shittin' crazy," he spat as he pulled off his voice changer and mask. "He confirmed the existence of one of the most secure vaults, *and* it's got shit we haven't even begun to imagine-"

"I know..." Asher interrupted, pulling off his own mask and changer. "...This changes things a bit." He stroked his chin as he contemplated his next course of action.

"Not even Ruat can give you the right kind of clearance, if this joker is speakin' the truth. At least, I don't think they can."

"So, what if we enlisted? Or at least me... I could spend the next few years moving through the ranks, proving myself a valuable asset to them."

"Asher, military advancement would take

decades to get you to the point where you could access them. Our friend here made it clear they have data on every citizen. That includes us. If you expressed interest in the vaults, it would immediately raise red flags. I mean, if he didn't blunder around like a bloody sod, we wouldn't even have confirmation that the vault exists. The mere fact we know it exists is a threat."

He was silent as he contemplated Thillans words. "Let's get out of here before he wakes. We need to get ready for our guests tomorrow anyways. Maybe having them here will help us come up with a plan."

Thillan shrugged as they threw off their hoodies and emerged from the office. Asher flipped a sigil to the barkeep, enough to generously pay for his cooperation in their dealings and for the mess they left. His mind immediately drifted to D'Vnora and Asher's wild plans, drowning out the sounds and smells around them as they made their way to the exit. He almost wanted to chuckle; Asher was a nutter...

...But Thillan wouldn't have it any other way.

Chapter 7

Ayela yawned and tried to stretch as best as she could in the passenger seat. Kamille, on the other hand, was busy typing her civilian ID into the dash's computer screen so the gatekeepers would open up. Sanctuary towns needed the added layer of security in case the crimes that the person committed were too heinous, even for towns like this one.

"What's your ID, love?"

Ayela yawned once more. "Two-seven-eight-v-l-twenty-two-thirty-nine," she answered sleepily.

A few seconds after she entered the codes, the gates creaked loudly and shifted open. Inside, the street lamps were nearing their last moments before they shut off for the day. Black roads lined with bleach-white sidewalks on either side stretched on into the town like a dark river. Cars casually drove by, crossing the road onto other streets while pedestrians stuck to the walkways. There were plenty of pauper citizens, dressed in the poverty they came from. They looked as one would imagine those fleeing from their pasts would look.

Every so often, they would see someone who looked like they came from a wealthier background, but most people looked like average, working-class citizens. Ayela always had a soft spot for the people of Shamol. Many of them were broken like her; orphans, outcasts, the wrongly accused. Many were victims of unfortunate circumstances. A lot of them lost loved ones, and even more were ostracized for beliefs and lifestyles. They were the ones that religious fundamentalists in positions of power disagreed with.

It didn't take long for Kamille to find the inn that the boys were staying in. It was a humble wooden building, smaller than any of the other apartments that filled their vision and obscured the horizon in the distance. It was well kept, cozy and contrite. Ayela had grown familiar with it over the last year with how often they would visit.

When she pulled the car over to the curb, Thillan quickly rushed out of the entrance with open arms. Kamille squealed with an excited, ear-piercing tone and practically jumped out of the driver's seat as she ran over to him. She jumped into his arms and kissed him with an intensity that one would expect from new lovers. It made Ayela smile...

...They weren't new lovers.

No, in fact, they'd been together since long before she met Kamille. The dark elf often went on to describe every facet of her man's character and physical description – even against Ayela's protest of more *explicit* details. It warmed her heart to see someone so in love after such a long time. There were plenty of stories and statistics that show just how easily couples fall apart in all countries. Her heart throbbed as she listened to their affectionate whispering and giggling, and she felt a twinge of pain as her mind drifted to Rhaja.

I miss you so much, she thought to herself. She wished she could hold her hand once more, kiss her lips, run her hand through her hair with the fiery romance they once indulged themselves in... She was confident that Rök kept her memory safe in the jar on his throne.

She took a deep breath and then got out of the car, and quickly made her way over to them. "Ayela, our crimson-haired princess!" Thillan exclaimed, pulling her in for a hug.

"Hey, Thillan," she said softly, returning his embrace. "How fares business in Shamol?"

"Oh, I'm sure you've assumed the usual; debauchery, crime, spilled secrets and plenty of drank ale... I'm sorry about what you two had to go through during congregation. I can imagine it was more than traumatizing," Thillan consoled.

She forced a thankful smile. "They'll be avenged... Their deaths won't be meaningless... Where's Asher?"

"Inside, up in our meeting room."

"Well let's not keep him waiting, babe. We can go off on our own after business is settled."

Thillan smirked and planted a kiss on Kamille once more. "Let's get to it, then."

The pub was crowded and felt older than time itself, planked with bright wooden walls and lights fashioned in scones for an ancient, Nordic aesthetic. The floors were covered by massive rugs under the seats and tables, while the bar was built on the far wall. On the side were the stairs that led to rooms only certain people had access to – among whom were the darklings. Patrons filled its massive hall with laughter, clanging of forks against plates, and plenty of delicious smells to accompany the tasty food and strong drink.

They made their way through, nodding at the bar-keep as they passed by, and ascended the stairway. There was a hall atop the stairs that led to three small bedrooms and the meeting room where Asher was waiting for them. Much to Ayela's surprise, the noise was muffled until it was almost inaudible in the upper rooms. It led for peaceful business to be conducted among anyone who had need of those spaces. For them, it was quite often, and they paid generously for the inn's services.

"Friends," Asher said as Thillan opened the door. He was smooth and silver-tongued, just as Kamille described him. It was Ayela's first time meeting the legendary leader of the darklings – or, at least, the only one who remained in contact with their leader. "Welcome. I know you've had a long journey."

"I'll say. Congregation went nuts, long journey after escaping a lockdown in a major hold – I can't imagine what you girls have been through."

"Thanks, Thillan," Ayela said. "It's been long indeed, but the day's still young, and we have a lot to go over and catch up on."

"She's not joking. We saw the whole fiasco with our own eyes, watched the emperor devolve on screen while he banned her religion – which could be more permanent than anyone would like, religious or not. He's displaying power that anyone would fear from a dictator."

"Then let's take a seat and get to work, everyone. We'll catch a couple drinks later tonight. The pub's left us the bar and the upstairs for as long as we need it after hours," Asher offered as he sat down at the large round table in the middle of the room. There were plenty of snacks, drinks, and coffee piled in the center for them to munch on and make drinks with while they discussed their plans – something that Ayela was accustomed to when any darkling cells met with each other. Historically, it was treated as a party to avoid suspicion by rather invasive law-enforcement, and eventually became a long-standing tradition.

They all took their seats, and Thillan piled his plate with plenty of cheeses and crackers to sate his appetite. She made herself some coffee while Kamille leaned against her lover. "I'll start," Asher began. "We interrogated an imperial official yesterday morning with information about one of the most highly secured data vaults in the empire."

Kamille's eyes widened with excitement. "You mean the vaults of D'Vnora are *real?!* It's no longer rumor and heresay?!"

"That's exactly what I mean," Asher responded. As smooth as his voice was, he maintained his lack of emotion when he spoke, perpetually sounding irritated with reality. "Our guest in Shamol was seen leaving from a very particular location in the slums of the city, and our *eyes* followed him here. No one really knows why, though."

"Did he perhaps have things he wanted to leak to the public?" Ayela proposed. Everyone was silent at her suggestion. "Or did we think about that? What *exactly* did you do to him?"

Kamille immediately looked at Thillan's knuckles and noted the scratches and scabs. "You *beat* him?!"

"He had info, and there was-"

"I assure you he had no intention of leaking data to anyone," Asher reassured. "His final words before we knocked him out were a threat that we wouldn't make it inside the vaults. Regardless, we have an idea now of what we're going to do, and it'll take all of us."

"Hold on, now; we have our own errands to run, boys. Ayela's congregation and the ban of Korism. We need to find out what's going on there... We need to find out what the empire's up to."

"I understand that, which is why I have a plan that benefits everyone. If the empire is behind whatever happened, I promise the information is stored on a server in this vault. We need to get in there. So, here's the plan," Asher began. "We need to get to D'Vnora, break into the vault, steal as much data as we can, and broadcast it from the central national news center in the capital. If everyone does as I say, we'll make it out with a treasure trove of information and leaks, and we'll weaken the imperial grip on this country so significantly, the nation won't have a choice but to elect new leaders and new imperial procedures. We will change this nation for the better."

"Okay... How?"

"It's not going to be easy, Ayela, but you're a very central part of this plan," Asher began.

Thillan smirked. "You're a dancer, right? So you can use your divine logic to get us into the vaults undetected."

"No! Absolutely not!" Kamille barked, standing up from her chair with such force, she nearly knocked it over.

"And why, oh leader of the darklings, should she not?" Asher spat in a condescending tone.

"Divine logic is detectable. We don't know the layout of the vaults. The empire is actively hunting divine logicians to *execute*. Not to mention the things that will happen to us if we're caught. This plan is already not going to work."

"Babe, you don't know any of that," Thillan complained.

"Asher, what happened when Ayela went ballistic in Sümol? What were the reports Karinth fed you?" Kamille demanded.

"Total lockdown of the facility and hold, and that the presence of an aethril-like entity was detected from satellite scans; divine logician is likely. Civilian evacuation of target sector imminent."

Kamille placed her hands on her hips and shifted her weight while she glared at her boyfriend. Ayela sipped her coffee, savoring its sweet, sugar-influenced flavor before clearing her throat. "Using my abilities to make us invisible to cameras and people doesn't take a lot of effort. It was one of the first things I experimented with when I was a little girl. Teleportation would trigger orbital scans, but not making someone invisible. I can cloak myself and anyone else as it's needed. I've done it plenty of times before without having the empire send their interrogators to come find me. And if this promises to reveal why those bastards in the Kult attacked so many congregations, I *want* to take that risk."

"You don't think that maybe – just maybe – this place would have ever greater measures in place to catch someone who can use divine logic?" Kamille pointed out.

Asher chuckled. "Divine logicians are so rare now, I doubt they'd plan for it. They nearly exterminated all of them. Ayela's among the last of her kind. So no, I don't think they have greater measures against people like her. Even if they do, she has no reason to hide herself at that point; she can break herself out with her abilities."

Kamille sighed in frustration, but before she had the chance to speak, Ayela reached over and grabbed her hand. "It's okay, Kamille. I can handle it. I'm a big girl."

"I know, but... You're one of my only friends-"

"Hey–"

"And I don't want to lose you like I've lost so many others... The empire's taken a lot from us all."

Ayela remembered her pain. Kamille shared how the empire targeted her city block one time because they thought there was an escaped convict in the area, and they opened fire on unsuspecting civilians. Her parents were among those killed. Her sister was ravaged and slaughtered by the very convict they were looking for days later, and nearly did the same to her before officers rescued her. Even younger than that, when she was a child, the empire arrested her uncle and executed his wife under suspicion of harboring Songrivan fugitives. They confiscated their belongings and seized their earnings at the bank. Thillan had it even worse than that.

"The empire won't take me. I promise," Ayela reassured. Kamille let out a long exhale and resumed her seat.

"You better keep that promise, love. I'll bring you back to life and beat you myself if I have to," Kamille threatened. Ayela snickered and sipped her coffee again.

"Alright, friends, let's start working out the details of this plan..." Asher began. Ayela's thoughts drifted to the future, attempting to predict what their desperate measures might yield for their success. So much has happened to all of them, she wondered how they were still able to go on fighting. Her heart still ached for Rhaja, but she was sure she would see her again in another life. She imagined how Kamille must have felt when her family was killed, or Thillan when he was tortured by the empire. She fantasized about Asher's childhood, how he wasn't even considered for an orphanage. He was left to wander the streets by himself and survive on his own.

How similar their stories were...

How alike they were to her...

Without friends or home, in an uncaring empire...

Chapter 8

The day progressed slowly until nightfall hit, and they were left with a table void of snacks, a bar below void of patrons, and a burning desire to enjoy each other's company with strong drink and meaningful conversation. They indulged in pints of ale and short glasses of liquor, and shared their deepest thoughts and wildest dreams while drinking away the harsh reality of their dark lives.

As they finished their fourth bottle of ale, though, Kamille and Thillan led each other up the stairs and into one of the rooms, kissing all the way up. Ayela smiled as she watched them, and went behind the bar to grab another bottle that she could enjoy by herself. "You know, culture would dictate a woman drinking this much by herself is unbecoming."

"I don't really care what culture thinks," Ayela spat with slurred words as she leaned against the bar. She was certainly drunk, but not to the point where she couldn't stand up straight. Reading was certainly difficult for her, though. "Culture said my folks'r are lesser than other elves."

"That's certainly not what we think. I hope you know that," Asher said in perfect form, as though he weren't even affected by the alcohol. "You have a good night, and don't stay up too late. We wake early tomorrow." With that, he stood up from the bar and made his way upstairs.

Ayela sighed and stumbled back over to her seat at the bar, then popped the cap off her bottle and took a heavy swig. She leaned her back against the bar and looked around at the empty room, wondering what it would have been like if she weren't given up by her parents. She wondered if she'd have ever gotten involved with groups like the darklings – or if her parents would have even taken her to Enthedrill to begin with.

She'd heard about Songrivan culture and architecture; it was beautiful and ethereal. There was an element to it that brought it out of the history books' pages, with cities built into forests, castles and pyres that towered over mountains, and elegant artwork built into every aspect of their way of life. They brought an entirely new meaning to elvish culture, and made her proud to have come from such strong and beautiful societies. The empire had its own aesthetic, for sure, but there was something about the way Songrivans wove their cities and societies into the nature around it that made her want to *be* there. She wanted to be with her people.

Then, as she took another swig of her ale, a shadowy figure loomed outside the entrance, peering in to find her by her lonesome and lost in her thoughts – which she was quickly pulled out of. She sobered up a little out of fear, and was ready for an attack. The figure didn't knock, though. Instead, it motioned for her to come over with a rushed wave of her hand. She hesitated at first, but she gave in and went over to the door. The figure held up her phone with a message that Ayela struggled to read;

I know you're heading to D'Vnora, and that you'll be stopping by Cassum on the way just before you get to the city. I'll meet you in Cassum in the alley behind Jagin's Bakery the night you arrive. Please be there. I don't believe in coincidences.

Perhaps it was the alcohol, perhaps it was Ayela's experience with the Kult, but whatever it was, she didn't feel the familiar numbness of fear or anxiety over her mysterious guest. She simply held a thumbs up in front of the window, and the figure ran off. As he was running away, though, she thought she caught a glimpse of a face that was severely beaten. Her thoughts drifted to the imperial the boys beat senseless, but then she chalked it up to the alcohol. She sighed and shut the lights off as she headed up the stairs. A good night's sleep is what everyone needed after everything that had happened. Whoever this stranger was, they could wait until the morning for her to pay any thoughts or attention towards. For now, she just wanted to drift off into the ocean of drunken dreams.

...Perhaps they would take her once more into Rhaja's loving embrace...

III

Episode 3

Tribes

Chapter 9

The sun peered through the blinders of her window, spewing rays of light in orchestrated columns through the maelstrom of dust in the air. Her head throbbed with intensity, and she wanted to yell at herself for not drinking enough water. She groaned as she tossed the sheets off and sat up, and rubbed her temples to try and alleviate some of the pain. Sighing, she put on her pants and threw her shirt over her tank top, and emerged from her room with squinted eyes.

"Bloody hell, love," Kamille giggled. Ayela hadn't even looked at her hair, but she knew it was a mess. "Let's get you some coffee. We'll pack your things in a little bit."

"Thanks," she groaned with a raspy voice.

"Let's not dally around too much, though," Asher said, handing Ayela her coffee before grabbing some more of the trash they left from the night before. She couldn't even imagine how he wasn't hungover. Thillan at least looked like everything was too bright and loud for him. Kamille, on the other hand, was chipper and perky, seemingly unphased from any pain she likely felt. Did Ayela really drink more than any of them? It didn't matter.

She sipped her coffee and took a seat at the table. One by one, the others did the same after pouring themselves some. "We know our plan," Thillan said with a smirk. "We're going to really hit the empire where it hurts."

"Let's make sure our phones aren't in the room before we start discussing anything," Asher ordered. They obeyed.

"Now that we're all clear, let's talk about the next few days," Kamille began. "We'll pass through the towns along the way quickly, but our driver won't stop until we reach Cassum. He asked that we help him with some business in town when we arrive, which I told him we *obviously* would."

"Naturally," Asher agreed.

"It's just a simple delivery. It's how he keeps his public front as a trucker. Once we finish helping him, we'll stay in Cassum for the night to go over our mission and objective details. Then, we enter the city and head to Asher's coordinates. Thillan will go and find a rendezvous point, and we will wait there until we're sure we can leave without setting off any alarms or triggers."

"Sounds great, babe, but who's going in with Ayela?" Thillan asked.

Kamille hesitated to answer for a few moments. "I'm not sure yet. We will make that decision when we need to."

"Agreed," Asher assured. "Sound plan, Kamille. Just like we talked about yesterday. Now let's pack up and go to the east gate. Our ride should be waiting for us now."

"Make sure to leave the keys to the car you drove with the bartender," Thillan said before kissing his lover and getting up from his seat.

With another cup of coffee in hand, her third one, they left the inn and made sure the bartender was paid in sigil and with the vehicle. The day was clear and bright, and the warmth of the sun created a perfect harmony with the brisk autumn breeze that passed through the town. Everything was calm and peaceful. Other people passed them by, their casual chatter filling her ears when they were close, while the sounds of cars driving by helped to fill the other voids of sound. The cool sensation of the air gently brushed her skin and aided the smell of the fresh outdoors in her nose. Slowly, the medicine she took and the caffeine she drank numbed the pain of her beaming hangover, and she was able to put herself together nicely and enjoy her day.

They walked for nearly forty minutes before arriving at the eastern gate, and as Kamille promised, their ride was waiting for them in a massive hauler with a long trailer hitched behind it. Their driver was a petite dark elf with greying hair, but she carried herself with the confidence of a young soldier. "You lot ready?" She asked with a thick accent similar to Thillan's. Ayela was sure the greying hair and slight wrinkles were more from the stresses of her job than anything else.

"Readier than ever," Kamille chirped.

"Good. You can throw your bags in the back room of the cab and make yourselves at home. This hauler was meant to house a family, so there's more than enough room. We'll be at Cassum in three-day's time, granted there aren't any detours."

Ayela turned to look at Shamol one more time, inhaling and exhaling deeply. If there ever was a home she could find in the empire, that town was it. She smiled, and then turned to enter the truck. The door shut behind her, and with roaring engines, the citizens around were made aware of the hauler signaling its departure.

When everyone was comfortable, Ayela looked through her bag for her phone and found an object wrapped up in paper dark enough to go unnoticed for as long as it had been. Curious, she pulled it out, ignoring the joking and casual conversation the rest of her friends were having, and gently unraveled the wrapping. It was a book with a note atop that read, *From your friend, Karinth.* She set the paper aside and smiled with misty eyes as she looked at the most beautifully designed Alldweii, her sacred scriptures. The cover was a deep indigo with golden trimming, and its pages were colored on the outside with a metallic sage. She swelled with emotion knowing she had such a good friend in him, and returned to the others with a thought repeating over and over in her head...

Thank you, Karinth...

Chapter 10

The port town was won for the Sovereignty. Kudaj reveled in his victory, and he watched as more troops poured in from Centerton. "Prince Kudaj," called out a commander from their reinforcements. He took a deep breath and turned to face him. "Imperial forces have retreated from the surrounding towns. We've secured this sector of Southton, and await further instructions."

"Reinforce Southton townships and cities. We need to make sure the nobles of the keep in Soton Forest are aware that the shores of the South can be opened again. Bolster the garrisons at the border and maintain defenses against imperial forces that have invaded Easton. House Carral should reach out with a message about their current situation soon," Kudaj ordered as he led the commander through the remains of the empire's fortifications. They'd spent the past week since their victory rebuilding the town and strengthening the walls the empire left behind. He used it as a base of operations, keeping minimal contact with his father. He didn't want to risk communicating on any line or frequency that wasn't secure.

"Yessir, your highness. Should we also deploy ships to some of the inland cities that have fallen to the invasion?"

"No. We need all the ships we have either engaging with the enemy fleet over the Latvian and Aspan oceans, or protecting our own shorelines. Send a message to Princess Elysianna Carral of Easton to ready her troops. Once we've secured and rebuilt Southton's fallen towns and cities, Centerton forces will deploy to Easton and rendezvous with her, where we can strategize out next course of action," Kudaj ordered. The commander nodded and quickly saw his own exit. The prince of Songriveii was left to his own thoughts as he surveyed the reparations he and his troops were making for the people of the nation he would one day inherit.

He was a mixture of emotions; pleased to see hope fill his people's faces once more, sadness that they had to suffer so, and incomparable wrath that the empire dared to engage in such a brutal war to begin with. He never forgot and never forgave – they murdered his sister. They deprived him of the memories and childhood he could have had. They robbed his family's future, and they murdered his only sibling.

It would continue to push him and drive him to war against Songriveii's invaders. It would force him to have nothing contempt for their fascist, power-hungry ruler. That hatred would burn in his heart until he saw *their* lands burn for the crimes they committed against his people and his family. He served his people to protect them from vicious monsters like them, and he continued to let that be the mantra and moral he organized his heart with.

"Lieutenant," he called out, signaling for the officer to make her way over to him.

"Yes, your highness."

"What's the status of the Weston garrisons?"

"I'm unsure, sir. It's possible they haven't deployed troops yet. A lot of their forces are occupied with the prison in the canyons of Olkimomno. A lot of maintenance is require to keep that prison functional," she revealed. He grunted. It wasn't what he wanted to hear, but there was nothing any of them could do about it. She was entirely right. If Weston lost anymore of Centerton's support, they would have vulnerability they could not recover from.

If the mechanical terrors of the canyons were loosed onto the continent, it would spell disaster for the nation. It was a cost too great. Not even divine logicians – being as rare as they were – could stand a chance against the remnants of the thousand-year blight, a time from long before the era of the daethrils. It was Songriveii's best kept secret from the public eye, and one of the only agreements between all of thaerv; the worst of the worst in every country could be sentenced to time in the prison. Even the empire, despite the war going on would send their worst prisoners there. If Kudaj had his way, the emperor would spend his life there.

"It's a bloody mess, that's for sure. What of the garrisons in Northton? Can they reinforce Easton?" He continued before handing off letters to some of the other officers in the command tent.

"A lot of them are stretched thin as it is. The ebony elves of Northton have been offering their naval might to the war overseas. They have ground forces, but many of them are reinforcing the border to Easton," she answered.

"Then we must do what we can to bolster South-ton's forces and make sure it's able to enforce its own borders. I had the commander of the reinforce-ments send a message to Easton's princess. I need you to send a message to Prince Locion of Southton; tell him to begin negotiations with Durinveii. Let's see if we can finally put our petty squabble with the dwarves behind us and work together to stop this threat," Kudaj ordered. The lieutenant saluted and quickly vanished.

Good...

Everything is turning out better than I'd hope.

Chapter 11

Ayela picked up another package their driver was delivering, reminiscing over the trip and everything that happened before. She spent the majority of their journey reading, despite everyone begging for her attention. She explained that it was nothing against them; it was just how she liked to spend her down-time. They entertained themselves with conversation, the hauler's built-in television, and occasional games on their phones. Everyone kept silent about their plans while they were around any sort of devices. There was a notable fear that the government was listening with each passing moment.

When they made it to Cassum, they were even more tight-lipped. There was no indication to who they could trust except for those they knew, and there wasn't the protection of the sanctuary town for them to take refuge under either. Here, they were on the field. They were every bit as exposed as they wished they weren't, and no matter what they did, it certainly felt like all eyes were on them.

Or at least, all eyes were on her.

She carried a heavier secret than the others; she was a dancer. A divine logician. It didn't help that she was so blatantly Songrivan that no one would question it when they looked at her; crimson locks, violet eyes, and the freckled, pale skin of a *blood elf*. To some, she was an exotic beauty that they had no hesitation objectifying. It made her want to wear baggier clothes and hide her figure from their ravenous gazes.

To others, she was a mutation in the reman race, a blight to all remankind. *That* made her want to do the opposite; to show a little more and prove them wrong. To prove to them that the beauty of the redheaded Songrivans of the Sovereignty was nothing to be ashamed of. It was a confusing place to be in, and it made her all-too aware of herself and her reality. If she let it, she would be a prisoner to society. She longed to fade into the background and be invisible to their sight. For some reason, though, Rök saw fit to make her stand out all-the-more.

"That's the last of it," Thillan said, emerging from the store. There were plenty of packages, boxes and pallets still in the trailer, but it was meant for another location.

"Yea, it certainly looks like it," their driver answered with a smirk. "It was fun, ladies and gents, but a girl's gotta make her runs. *Stick to the shadows, ye huddled foes."*

"And in the shadows, they secrets be known," Kamille said with a smile as she took her friend's hand and pulled her in for a hug. "Stay safe out there."

"You too, Kamille. You still got friends in Shustur. Don't forget it."

Then the driver made her way to the cab and climbed into the driver's seat. As the truck started to move, they all waved goodbye and waited for her to disappear in the distance. "Alright, everyone," Asher began. "Let's head to hotel. We're a not that far away, so we should be there in no time."

"Actually, there's a bakery I wanted to stop by before heading to the hotel. I hope you don't mind," Ayela lied. Her meeting with the stranger from Shamol hadn't left her mind since that night.

"You're a bit of a nutter, wanting to haul all of this to a bloody bakery *then* go to the hotel," Thillan complained.

"No, that's fine. You can go there yourself, just meet us at the hotel in an hour," Asher agreed. Ayela sighed, relieved.

"Thanks. I appreciate it," she said. "I'll catch up with you guys."

"Don't be gone too long," Kamille called out as Ayela diverged from the group. She waved back at them before getting lost in the thickening crowds.

Cassum was a bustling town with more people than it seemed to have room for. It made sense, of course; it was a border town to the hold of D'Vnora. It was one of the most decrepit cities in the nation, and there were still plenty of people who couldn't even afford to get through the front gates. Oftentimes, they ended up in Cassum as a permanent resident, with or without a home.

Unlike Shamol, the people here were desperate and afraid of the wilds. Paranoia often influenced daily life in this town, and they behaved as such. People regularly treated everyone around them as though they were trying to pick a fight. It was often rather frightening.

She was used to environments like this, though. She learned to keep her head low and her hood up when needed. The crowds were louder than in Shamol, and there were too many cars driving around. Some people walked their pets, which added an additional layer of stress. Every gaze from a passerby made her uncomfortable, and the smells that wafted by her nose were horrendous. It took time for her to get used to it, but when she arrived at the bakery, the smell of freshly baked bread replaced the town's stink quickly.

Making sure no one else was following her, she

vanished in the alley behind the bakery as she was directed. Initially, there was no one there, and she was about to walk away in frustration until she heard someone clear their throat from the other side of the dumpster and trash bags piled all around.

Ayela turned and was faced with a woman about her height with bright, light-purple eyes and black locks cut into a shoulder length bob. Her pale complexion was easy to look at, and despite her poor clothes, she looked as though she kept herself clean and kept. Immediately, she felt she could trust this girl. There was something about her that put her mind at ease.

"Hello, Ayela," she said with a soft and gentle voice. "My name's Kacyn. I'm a Songrivan like you."

That much was clear. Her accent was thick Songrivan, like the natives of Northton that she probably hailed from. "An Ebony elf," Ayela declared, examining her from head to toe. "It's even harder to find one of you here than it is my kind."

"Blood elves and Ebony elves hail from the same ancestors, Ayela. It's only natural we're drawn to one another when we're in foreign lands... Especially when both of us are divine logicians," Kacyn revealed. Suddenly, all other sounds were muffled, and her body went numb. All she could see in her increasing tunnel vision was Kacyn.

Another divine logician?

"W-What do you mean? You're saying you're a divine logician too?" Ayela stammered.

"I do... Though, we're not *entirely* the same. You're a dancer – one of the strongest of our kind. I'm a farseer."

"*Farseer?*"

"That's right," Kacyn confirmed. "My variant of divine logic is called *Vision.* You have *Space-time.* There's a trove of information about our kind in the libraries of Northton... And despite the war, news travels fast around the globe."

Ayela felt floored. She felt as though she'd been lied to her whole life. "Wait, you mean to tell me there's been someone like me this *whole time,* and I never knew it?!"

"The empire has lied to you most of all, Ayela. The Sovereignty is home to many divine logicians, though none as powerful as you... Dancers are among the rarest born. Only one is known in our country; Prince Kudaj of the royal family. Many of us seek to restore the order of the Yglsora... Some even want the Uri'Kai variant to return..."

"...Is that why you're here?" Ayela guessed. Kacyn's eyes lit up at her question, and a smile tugged at her the corners of her mouth.

"Can you read minds too? Is there no limit to the power of the dancers?" She asked excitedly.

"No, but it only makes sense... But how can I trust you? Accents are easy to replicate, and the empire can certainly use makeup and surgery to imitate an Ebony elf."

Kacyn smirked. She looked into Ayela's eyes with an intensity, and she started to notice her new friend's eyes glowing. "I see the facets of your tired spirit rippling and radiating like a flower waiting to blossom with love. I see the pain of your childhood and your life keeping that budding spirit sealed tight, waiting for the right trigger to open its overflow of emotion... I see your abandonment at the orphanage, your youth and adolescence spent in dojos and dance halls to hone your divine logic and channel your mighty power, your heart yearning for the love of your late lovers, and your questions about your heritage... I also see a closer connection to your god than you yourself even see-"

"No offense, but these are past events that, with enough research, anyone can find-"

"-I see the spirit of Rök enveloped around you like the wings of a white bird, marking one who has been touched by *Hashem*." Kacyn finished. Ayela felt the blood drain from her face at the mention of the name... It was a name for Rök she'd received in meditation. It was years ago, before she'd ever met Rhaja, or her boyfriend prior to Rhaja. She never shared that name with anyone. She was confident no one would know what it meant, but here was someone she'd never met before telling her the name like it were a common fact that everyone was aware of.

Ayela was convinced.

"...You want to revive the Uri'Kai?" She finally asked after moments of silence.

"Yes and no... I want to start something from its ashes. You and I, we can start anew. We can use a name from the earliest settlers of this country; *The Tribes of Enthedrill*," Kacyn answered excitedly. "You know the names of the tribes?"

"Of course; Majjai, Emira, Siphon, Sa'Alah, Xadokk, Ki'Tsun, and Tsana. Seven tribes that fought off the machines of the thousand-year blight. Siphon and Sa'Alah helped establish Songriveii before returning to Enthedrill, and Majjai founded the city of Bavylune," Ayela answered, reciting her history lessons.

"That's right... Let's revive the Uri'Kai through the Tribes of Enthedrill. You and I will start with the two main tribes. You can take the name of Majjai, and I will take the name Emira. Together, we can revive the order and keep the peace of thaerv like they did so long ago," Kacyn pleaded. She was clearly unable to contain her excitement, and Ayela found it adorable.

There was truth in what she was saying, though; the Uri'Kai had been gone for too long, and they had the means of restoring the dead order. It was right within their grasp. She believed in the cause Kacyn presented, and wanted to grow in her abilities with others who were like her.

But there were other things that needed to come first.

The congregation came to mind.

The banning of Korism came to mind.

The Towlålites came to mind.

Most importantly, her friends came to mind.

"You don't need to say anything; I saw it all. Your mission, your friends, and the things you're up against... If you are Majjai, you are going to be our leader. As such, I will follow your lead," Kacyn declared. Ayela hesitated, but before she could speak, her new friend read her mind again. "I know they won't trust me at first. That's okay. Just introduce me and protect me, and they will warm up to me. I need you to keep the Tribes a secret between us, though. This must be the greatest of secrets... Please..."

Ayela took a deep breath. "Alright, Kacyn. I trust

you. I'll keep this just between us. When the time is right, you and I will start to look for other divine logicians and accept them into the Tribes," she agreed. Kacyn squealed and embraced Ayela. With a smile on her face, she followed her friend back to the others...

And Ayela struggled to figure out a way to explain everything to them...

Chapter 12

The hotel room was larger than expected; two beds in a bedroom, an entirely separate living room with a couch that had a pullout bed, a bathroom and a small kitchen. There was even a table that could seat the five of them, which was where Ayela found each of them sitting and staring at her and Kacyn in disbelief. She expected it to be worse than it was, if she were being honest.

"...This girl is another divine logician like you, from Songriveii, and knew of our plans and wants to help?" Asher restated. Ayela exhaled all of her anxious tension.

"I stand by what I said."

"And we're just supposed to trust you two? You realize that it looks as though you broke away from us to specifically meet with this girl, right?" He pointed out. She hid her flustered expression well. He was too accurate in his guessing. "Why should we trust her? We trust you well enough, which is why we didn't outright deny any ties to you, but this is a stranger."

She wanted to tell them everything, but kept her mouth shut. She wanted to tell them about the stranger at the pub, but she wasn't sure how they'd react. She was stuck in a place where she was lost, unsure of her next action or the results of any decision she would make. Then, in her moment of distress, Kacyn gently placed a hand on her arm and smile warmly.

"It's okay, Ayela," she cooed.

That was all the confidence she needed.

"There was a stranger at the pub in Shamol after you all went to bed. I couldn't see any details, but he stood outside the door and waited for me. When I approached, he held up a phone with a message from Kacyn telling me to meet her alone. So, I needed to make sure I'd truly be *alone,* and I kept it a secret from you guys. I know you all well enough; you'd have followed me and watched from a distance," she explained.

Thillan snickered. "You're not wrong, I'll give you that."

"And if this were some sort of trap, it's better I be alone when it was sprung. If all of us were caught, the darklings would lose their strongest leadership. So, I went and met her. At first, I was as skeptical as all of you. Then she told me something that I'd never told anyone before... Something I kept very close to my heart... And because of that, because she was able to tell me that secret so plainly, she won my trust," she finished explaining. The others wore their contemplation like masks, and after a few tense and silent minutes, Asher stood to his feet.

"Then she will have a chance to prove herself and her abilities to us as well," he began. Kacyn threw up her hands in protest.

"Please, I know I can't change your mind in what you're about to say, but know that I would never cross a dancer. Their kind is so powerful, I would be a fool to challenge one. Our own prince levels battlefields with his power against your empire. With your challenge, keep that in mind. Ayela is your guarantee that I am no threat, even if I wanted to be," she explained. Kamille kept her stern expression, but stood up and approached her.

"Make sure you take care of our crimson princess here, or she won't be the only threat you have to worry about," she warned. Kacyn gulped.

"Great. Now that we're done threatening everyone, Kacyn is the one who will go with Ayela to steal the data," Asher said. "If she's as she says, her abilities will come in handy more than anyone else. Kacyn, you steal the data for us, you're one of us. That's my test. If you betray us, we make sure you pay for it."

Kacyn smiled, and Ayela was sure she was glad to finally be among friends...

IV

Episode 4

Vaults

Chapter 13

Poverty.

Violence.

Drugs.

Murder.

Those were some of the words used to describe one of the largest, filthiest holds in the nation. D'Vnora was an incubator of poverty and crime that went unrivaled in the empire. There were two levels to the sprawling metropolis; an entire upper area built on massive plates and platforms suspended above the poorer sectors that were built into a massive crater as ancient as society itself. Standing at the huge entrance to the walled city, one could see the two levels as though they were looking at a portrait showcasing their vast differences.

Above, it looked like there was life and bustling activity fit for the richest of society – and that truly was who lived in the upper levels. Corporate executives, those who inherited wealth, big business owners, and all the massive corporate entities one could find in a city dwelt on the plates. Down below, there were street gangs, crime syndicates, government housing. It was such a divide in society, that it was sickly poetic the way the city was structured.

They would often see personal airships and hovercars zooming by overhead, while ground cars like the one they all rode in continued along its dusty dirt path. Both halves of the city erected tall buildings and had hovercraft buzzing around them like insects, but while the city above was polished and glistened with reflected light from the sun, the city below was dull and brown like the dirt it was all set into.

Traveling farther into the undercity, they looked around at the people and saw familiar emotions draped over their faces. They were suddenly reminded why they were doing what they did; that it wasn't their fault for ending up where they were. It wasn't their fault for being born into an unforgiving and selective empire that valued stereotypes and vain image it longed to obtain more than the lives it was responsible for.

There were many Songrivans and dark elves like Ayela and Kamille living among the poor class of the undercity, and they all looked angrier than ever at the lives they were forced to live. Her heart broke when she looked at their faces, and she wished so badly she could do something about it. Every so often, she would see the mocha-colored skin of a dwarf wandering among them, and she was reminded of Rhaja. How would her late lover feel if she were there? She assumed her heart would break as hard as hers did.

It wasn't too long before they arrived a few blocks away from where Thillan's coordinates were. They exited the cab and quickly made their way into the run down hotel they planned to set up their base in. "My friend rented a room under the name Kaothin," Asher declared to the man at the front desk.

"Sure. Here's the room key. Next time, come before noon, yeah?" Came the curt and rude response. Asher ignored him and took the key.

The elevator seemed to take too long to reach their floor, and the journey to their room felt like hours when it was only minutes. The time for her to do what she'd never dreamed of doing before was close at hand; she was going to break in to one of the government's most secured facilities. She explored fantasy after fantasy of what new story and secret she would stumble across.

Entering the room, they quickly smashed their phones and set their bags down on the bed. Thillan was there waiting for them, as their plan dictated.

The men quickly set up all their secure equipment, safe from the government's prying ears and eyes. The girls were handed ear pieces connected to a secure line, closed off from any frequency that would be easily detectable.

"Here's the plan," Kamille began. "You two are going to get into the vault. Once you're in, since Kacyn is the mental one, she'll glean schematics of the facility from the guards or someone, and lead you to the data servers. This is very important; I'm giving you a device Asher was given from Ruat that can tap into government servers at most – if not, all – locations across the country and in foreign bases. There are programs installed that we don't even understand, but they're so user friendly that you don't need to be a tech-genius to figure out how to use them."

"Ruat... Spirit of the ancient creator... The feminine aspect of the maker-god. It's ironic your leader would pick such a name. I assume they have never shown themselves to you before?" Kacyn asked.

"That's correct," Asher answered honestly. "There's never been a need before, so we don't try to look for them. We just go to our next target when they give it to us."

"But this time, they didn't give you the target... You picked it yourself," Kacyn intuitively pointed out.

"...That's right."

Ayela wasn't entirely sure how to feel about this sudden revelation, or whether she should care. Perhaps there was a reason Asher was after it so badly, and that reason ultimately benefitted the darklings. Or perhaps it was an entirely selfish abuse of power. Regardless, she felt in her heart that infiltrating this vault was in line with her own goals, and no matter how selfish or selfless the reasons, it would benefit the darklings and bring the truth of the empire to the public.

"This vault holds secrets to bring down the empire," Asher began, answering Ayela's thoughts. "It's a center of wealth that the empire holds dear to its heart, and it holds truths that I personally need to confirm for myself. It holds something for Ayela and her religion. It holds something for those that were in Kamille's and Thillan's life's circumstances. This vault has something for us individually *and* collectively. We were given the means for opportunities just like this one, so let's take advantage of it."

"Right," Kamille continued. "Getting back on track; you'll plug the jack from this device into one of the servers, download as much data as you can hold or until the alarms are triggered. Once you're done, get out and rendezvous with us so we can take a look. As soon as we've gotten a good idea of what we have, we'll take a heavy hitter to Bavylune and broadcast it across the nation."

"When we reach Shamol, Thillan will stay in the town. After we finish in the Capital, I'll depart with the rest of the data to deliver to every cell in every town and city with broadcasting power strong enough to reach a wide radius around it, and we will spend the next few years leaking secret after secret. We'll take the empire's crutches from under them, and we'll get it ready for the collapse of this weak and tyrannical government," Asher declared with a clenched fist. She saw it in that moment; just how deeply he *hated* the empire.

"Let's get to it, then," Ayela said with a smirk.

Chapter 14

The destination wasn't far from the hotel. Both Kacyn and Ayela were dressed in all black, from their pants and hoodies to the shoes on their feet. She took a deep breath and looked over at her new-found friend, who offered a reassuring smile. "I'm ready whenever you are, Majjai," she encouraged. Ayela took a deep breath and watched the entrance to the building Asher claimed was the location of the vault. On cue, a woman carefully checked her surroundings and quickly disappeared into the entrance.

That was their chance.

She started to twirl her thumb around in a circular motion while her hands were in her hoodie pocket, and with the slightest flex of her divine logic, she was sure they were completely invisible to both person and camera alike. They ran quickly, careful to avoid the cars that couldn't see them, and approached the door as they slipped through the crowd unnoticed.

Kacyn opened the door carefully, sure that no one was paying attention, and the two of them quickly and quietly caught up to the woman that entered earlier. Ayela didn't need to concentrate too hard, but their sounds were only barely muffled, and if they were to interact with anyone, the person they touched would be alerted to their presence. Everything needed to go off without a hitch.

The inside of the building seemed simple enough at first; stained walls and dusty floors with a front desk that an older woman sat behind. A security personnel stood off to the side at the entrance that was armed with an assault rifle. The one they were following, though, was waiting patiently in front of an elevator. They snuck up as quietly as they could, but one unlucky step that Ayela took caused one of the wooden planks in the floor to creak loudly, stealing the attention of the others at their location.

Ayela's body went numb, but when Kacyn grabbed her hand, she remembered they couldn't see them. She kept her thumb twisting robotically, and they remained invisible. After a few moments, both the other women returned to their activities, and they continued to quietly tiptoe towards their target. The guard kept staring at the location of the sound, but didn't notice when they moved away from it.

Once they caught up, the elevator dinged and the

doors slid open. Inside, it was elegant and entirely too intricately designed for the slums of D'Vnora, confirming that they were in the right place. They mirrored the woman's clacking steps to mask their own, and followed her onto the platform as the doors closed behind them.

Dread overcame Ayela when she saw how many floors they needed to descend, but as her friend had done before, Kacyn calmed her anxious thoughts with a gentle smile and softly grabbing her hand. Ayela sighed quietly, and acknowledge her friend when she held up her pointer finger. *Floor 1. How convenient.* She thought to herself. It almost seemed too convenient, but she didn't question their luck.

After a long, 5 minute commute, the elevator abruptly stopped and the doors opened once more. They slipped out as quickly as they could and made sure to stay out of the woman's way, and remarked the long, dimly lit hall that seemed to stretch on for kilometers and kilometers in either direction. They let their unknowing friend vanish down the hall as the clacking of her heels continued to echo long after she was gone.

Ayela made sure there wasn't anyone else around before letting out a sigh of relief. *"Did she have a layout of this place in her head?"* She asked. Kacyn nodded with a beaming smile.

"Indeed. Follow me. There are servers on this level that have access to many of the secrets we'd need to incriminate the empire. The lower levels are too risky for us, and even if we made it to them, we'd never make it out. This is our best bet," she answered.

Kacyn led her in the opposite direction the woman went, and they hastened their steps the further away they got. It seemed like they were in an endless loop, but eventually, they started to come across doors on either side of the hall, and they made more of an effort to soften the sounds their running.

"We're close," Kacyn whispered, pointing to a door that was only a little farther down the hall. They quickly made their way over, but when they arrived, Ayela noticed a hand-scanner beside the doorway.

"Shit!" She swore. *"There's no way we can get in without a hand-print."*

"Wait patiently. Someone will come when at the right time."

So they did.

They waited.

And waited.

And waited.

Ayela wasn't sure how much time had passed, but it certainly felt like too much. She alternated between fingers she used to keep her power flowing, but eventually she would grow tired if they didn't find a quicker way of entry.

Then, she heard the clacking of heels that had grown all-too familiar. They looked back the way they came to find the same blonde-haired woman from earlier casually approaching from down the hall. Kacyn wore a beaming smile.

"Our someone has come," she whispered. They silently slid to either side of the door as the woman pressed her hand against the sensor, and then it obediently slid open. The girls followed her in as closely as they could, careful not to touch her or brush up against her, and nearly blew their cover in awe at the technological beauty of the airlock that led to the server room.

"Please enter identification," a robotic voice ordered over speakers as they continued forward.

"Ynsigna Lorrin," she called out. Not once did she look up. Not once did she break her stride.

"Confirmed. Welcome, Ynsigna Lorrin Aberthost. Rank priority level affirmed. Ynsigna access granted. Tread carefully and apply safety protocols around equipment. Have a wonderful day," the auto-voice declared.

The doors to the server room opened, and the girls were stunned when they stepped through. The Ynsigna had already vanished in a forest of cabling and towering servers arranged strategically in the dome-shaped chamber. A massive cooling fan spun atop, offering a wintery chill and filling their ears with noise they weren't expecting to be so loud.

"We must act quickly. The Ynsigna is needed to exit this room. Come with me," Kacyn said before dashing through the servers. She was a little more careless with how loud they were, considering they could easily mask their steps with the fan.

She followed the Ebony elf to a server in the center of the room, and looked around cautiously while Kacyn inserted the device's jack into the port. A green light beside it shifted red, and the screen on the device lit up, and Kacyn navigated through its interface flawlessly. Before they knew it, data was being copied onto its hard drive.

"No matter what happens, don't panic," She warned. Ayela's heartrate kicked up a little. Why would she need to panic?

Then, the Ynsigna walked past them, nearly bumping into Kacyn. Her heart jumped into her throat, and she nearly forgot to keep her fingers moving. Slowly, the worst possible situation seemed to be coming to fruition, and she cursed their ill-fated luck.

Just when she thought they were safe, though, Lorrin stopped dead in her tracks and turned around. Even with as far away as she was, her confusion was an evidenced expression on her face, and it was a signal of fear for Ayela. "Don't panic," Kacyn cooed. *How can you stay so calm?! We're about to be caught!* She thought to herself.

"Don't. Panic."

Closer.

Lorrin slowed her pace, nervous that something was wrong, and looked around. Paranoia set in: their situation was getting worse.

Closer.

The imperial officer took another step and twisted around, as if to get a better angle.

Closer.

The meter on the device was millimeters away from completion, and the percentage read ninety-nine.

Then the device flashed its screen and Kacyn quickly pulled the jack from the port. The light on the server immediately shifted green, and the farseer smoothly slid out of the way as Lorrin reached her hand out to feel around the light, as if to make sure the tower wasn't overheating in anyway. Satisfied that nothing was wrong, she shrugged and made her way to the entrance.

Ayela sighed in relief, and the two of them followed the officer out of the room and back into the hall. Lorrin predictably retraced her steps towards the elevator, and the dancer realized they were going to escape from the vaults with the treasure trove of data that Asher promised. It almost seemed too perfect. She was expecting something to go wrong at any moment.

When they arrived at the hidden entrance to the vault, having followed Lorrin all the way out, they dashed back across the street, and Ayela released them from their invisibility with a relieved sigh. She squealed excitedly and pulled Kacyn in for a tight hug, still in disbelief that they pulled it off without anything going wrong.

The farseer returned the embrace with a warm smile, and they relished in their victory despite the awkward looks they received from passerby's. "I can't believe that worked! Gods, I could kiss you right now!"

"While I certainly am flattered, I wouldn't want to put you in a compromising position-"

"Not like that, silly!" Ayela chuckled as she pulled away. Her heart was pounding in her throat from all the adrenaline, and she couldn't wait to get back and tell the others. Before she could say anything else, though, Kacyn's smile suddenly faded from her face, and fear filled her expression. "What's wrong?"

"I sense a dark presence... So dark... So cold... It's a presence that feels as though the stars of the universe themselves had died, and brought that death to thaerv," she explained. The blood drained from Ayela's face.

...Tallie.

"Let's get out back to the others," she said, grabbing Kacyn's hand and walking faster than she'd ever walked before. She kept her head on a swivel, and with anxiety watched every blonde-haired woman they passed by.

Not here.

Not now.

They couldn't have found her so quickly.

She refused to believe the Kult of Salom'Sileyu had found her again so quickly...

Chapter 15

They spent days combing through the data they retrieved. Not a single alarm was triggered. No soldiers came in waves to see who had stolen their information. No officials began to interrogate civilians to see if they were following rumors of the vault. It was eerie how easy it was for them to steal as much data as they did.

But there they were, with a collection of articles and documents tied to events they didn't even consider to have had government involvement. Every so often, one of them would show their findings to the others, but nothing caught Ayela's attention more than an encrypted file called 'Warlock.' Try as hard as she might, there was no way for her to crack the password or figure out a way to unlock it. Even Asher, the most tech-savvy of the five of them, wasn't able to figure it out.

She copied the file onto her own personal drive, resolving to bring it to Karinth on a later day to see if he could get it open. It wasn't long after that when she noticed a plan titled "Subjecation Event" with URGENT stamped across the front side of the folder in the image. Curious, she opened the file and quickly scanned through it, finding the data she was looking for. She exhaled all of the anxiety and tension built up in her lungs, and copied the file onto her thumbdrive.

"It's here," she declared. Everyone quickly clambered all around her, shoving the chairs over and even spilling a class of water onto the floor. "*Subjecation Event.* It details a plan to eradicate all religions except for a select few for the purpose of subjecting imperial civilians under totalitarian rule, and igniting a second warfront with Durinveii and possibly Dominov. It details planted agents across the nation that will be seen on camera as Durinveii operatives. They're even given false identities for the autopsy report to authenticate claims that Durinveii planned a military op, all so that Enthedrill can invade and conquer them as well as Songriveii. If Dominov ceases trade allegiances with the empire, they will be included in a third warfront... This is the biggest conspiracy we've ever-"

As she spoke, screams were heard from the streets down below. They rushed to the window and peered through as best as they could. There, in the middle of the street blocking all traffic and demanding the attention of the passerby's, was a dwarf with explosives strapped all over his torso. They all felt how that scream sounded; anxious, paranoid, panicked. Ayela's heart jumped into her throat, and she hesitated with what to do next.

He was a young man, caramel-colored skin with dark, cropped hair. He was barely taller than Asher, but looked like he'd had his whole life ahead of him. She couldn't see into his eyes from that distance, but she wondered if he'd regretted ever aligning himself with the empire. As if to answer her pondering, though, Kacyn placed a hand on hers and looked into her eyes with a mournful expression.

No.

The answer was no.

This dwarf had no regrets. In fact, he was convinced he was giving aid to the greatest thing that ever happened to him in his life. Before she had the chance to intervene, though, a powerful explosion rocked the apartment and threw them away from the window. They groaned as they slowly sat up, each of them with cuts and bruises likely forming under their clothes.

It was happening.

Just as she found the answer, they all watched it unfold before their very eyes. The congregations. The operatives. The conspiracy. It was to subjugate the world under a single empire with a single tyrant at its helm. They found the answer only when it was too late to stop it. Tears fell from her eyes, and her heart burned with a flurry of different emotion. *Why do men in power care so little for the lives they hold power over?* She thought to herself in despair.

...Is there any hope at all? Truly?

V

Episode 5

Terrorists

Chapter 16

It took the day for them to carefully escape the city amidst the chaos. Law enforcement was interrogating everyone in the vicinity. With the Kult still at large and their motives unknown, they couldn't risk being caught. They made sure to reach the edge of the undercity before hiring a cab to Cassum. Once they made it, though, they rented their same room from before and settled in for a restless night of anxiety and confusion.

Ayela laid there on the pullout with Kacyn beside her, the two of them wide awake and unable to get their minds off of what happened. "You felt a dark presence... I have to ask, do you know anything about cults and secret societies?" She asked. She glanced over at Kacyn, who seemed lost in her own thoughts.

"I know of the Kult of Salom'Sileyu from your own memories... And from other things. But that's not a tale for right now," she answered. Ayela became suspicious, glancing over at her with a furrowed brow and flattening her lips.

"Why not, exactly?" She asked.

"It's not time for you to hear that."

"As Majjai, I command you to tell me-"

"No, Ayela. You're not acting as the leader of the Tribes ought to act. There are things that I've seen that need to happen before you're ready for that. There are ways that you need to grow... Using a title and position to extort knowledge is... *Wrong*," Kacyn protested. Ayela paused and contemplated her statement. She was right. If she were going to be better than the Kult, she needed to enter a role of leadership with humility. If the divine logicians were to return to the world in any fashion, they needed to be trustworthy, not abusive. Her glancing and giving into distrust the that way she did was unbecoming of herself. She'd learned not to take everything at face value, but she also needed to learn where to draw the line and respect people's boundaries.

"I'm sorry," she said. "That wasn't right for me to do."

"It's okay, Majjai," Kacyn said with a smile. "You will know soon enough..."

Ayela could hear it in her voice. There was a slight tone that betrayed the regret she felt in her heart. There was a burning sensation in her chest that told her Kacyn wasn't entirely truthful about where she'd come from. Certainly, the accent was thick enough and natural enough to *feel* like she was a native Songrivan, and she had enough knowledge of their people and leaders. But she could have been hiding a very dark past that intertwined with the Kult somehow. Ayela was apprehensive, but she reminded herself that if Kacyn wanted to turn her in to the Kult, she'd have done it by now. There was no reason to help them get as far as they did...

She hoped...

Her eyes grew heavy, and she didn't resist the urge to close them and let her consciousness drift into the void before dreams filled her unconscious reality. There was a lot that had happened, and she wasn't sure what their next step was going to be, except to take their files to the capital. Her objective in mind, she coursed through her subconscious and entertained dreams of a day when the empire was no longer a threat to society...

Chapter 17

"Multiple attacks were reported all across the nation to-day as Durinveii natives planted themselves as suicide-bombers near both obscure locations and important government facilities. Casualties reported as great as the attacks on Korist ministers and law enforcement congregant members just weeks ago. The Emperor has released a statement from the throne this morning with an important message:"

"Durinveii has launched an attack on our very soils this day. We will not delay in an equally effective counter-attack against them. I know my citizens well. I know you all agree when I say that an attack against one of us is an attack against us all. Our forces will be divided and will advance on our new enemies with the same zeal and ferocity we have engaged in against those dogs of Songriveii. Lend a hand as best as you are all willing and able, and we will defend this land of sovereignty as the beacon of civility and society that it is. As it was written in the Alldweii, for you faithful among us; "The tiers of war have ascended among us. It is our responsibility to seeks its end, and bring peace to all under the control of Rök."

"...Wow. What do you think of that inspiring speech from the Emperor, Kadens?"

"I have to say, our emperor truly knows how to rally his people, even in the midst of this crisis where we now face a war on two fronts. There you have it, viewers; the three biggest super-powers in the modern age going head-to-head in a war bigger than any fought before. We-"

Asher shut the television off and tossed the remote onto the couch while the rest of them contemplated everything they'd just heard. "There we have it, darklings," he began. "The confirmation of everything we just read. A conspiracy of our government unravelling right before our eyes like a scene out of a film. We couldn't have seen any more terrifying a truth; this Emperor and his officials seek to rule the modern world... For what? Power? Glory? Money? To be the wealthiest ruler, or to be the one who said 'I did it!' to those that came before him? We have the chance to stop one of the stealthiest, most charismatic oppressors from seating himself to a position of power that he doesn't belong. And Ayela, for him to quote a text so precious to you, I know that burns in your heart like a raging fire that can't be quenched. Will you sit by while this shitty leader continues to abuse your god and your faith?"

She wasn't hiding it. Her brow was furrowed. Anger twisted her expression, and she wanted to march to the capital and rip his ivory tower apart with every ounce of divine logic in her being. Her senses were heightened, and her hands robotically curled into fists.

"Kamille and Thillan, your lives have been lived in paranoia, always looking over your shoulders. Will you sit by while others like you have their voices silences, unable to stand up for themselves against the empire?" He pressed on.

Thillan cleared his throat. "We've been in this from the start, Asher. You don't need to remind us why we're doing this. It'll only make us angrier."

"That's the point, my friend. I *want* you all to be angry. That rage means you won't back down when they threaten you. It means you won't forget what they did to you when they beg you for mercy. We don't have to take their lives to hit them where it hurts – we just have to make sure we don't miss."

She heard what Asher said, but she couldn't find it within herself to agree with him. He wanted to use their rage and their hurt as weapons. She wanted to be free of it all. If she was hurting, She would accomplish nothing in her actions but hurt more people. "You don't need to do that to us," she said. "We're plenty angry. We don't need more of it. We just need to act. We need to stop the empire before they do more harm. We have something in our corner that can do some real damage; let's use it before it's too late."

"I agree with her," Kamille said as she stood up. "What are we doing while we're sitting around here, pissing ourselves off at what the empire's done? Let's start off with a plan. Ayela and Kacyn, you two go back through and divvy up the data between two groups. We talked about Asher leaving for other cities and towns with information? So let's give him the bulkier data cluster. As for us, we'll take the other bit for the Capital like we planned. Let's try to get ahead of them and release any other plans they haven't acted on while it's still fresh."

Asher smirked and nodded. "Solid plan. Let's get to work. Divide the data, and we'll leave for Shamol tonight."

They spent the rest of the day hard at work. Two harddrives were loaded with projects and leaks. One was given to Asher, as planned, while the other was given to Kamille. Ayela refused when she revealed the drive she had in her pocket, and insisted her friend take it since it was her plan to begin with.

Before she began to pack her things, though, Ayela stumbled across another project that caught her undying attention, titled 'Project: Gathering.' Opening it, she found information on three pyramids that were discovered; one in the north pole, one in the south, and the final in the center of the mountain ranges in the Desert of Rök. The reports described them radiating with the same strange energy often detected when aethrils and divine logicians appear, and confirmed that they weren't built by remans...

They have existed since before elves ever evolved into being.

She furrowed her brow as she scrutinized the data, deeply analyzing every sentence. Three temples since the dawn of the world. One was home to the gods of the first elves, one was to the daethrils – the fallen gods – as old as the first, and the final was described as a temple impassable by any without the permission of the highest creator-god.

Whoever wrote the report believed the pyramid was constructed in an alternate universe, one far older than the one they existed in, and was fused with thaerv upon its formation. The title was what unsettled her the most; 'The Temple of Rök.' It wasn't the strange nature of the pyramids described in the project that frightened her, nor that the temples appeared to have been constructed before the dawn of time. No, it was that the empire knew about these things, and still willingly attacked faithful adherents to her religion.

Perhaps those who were attacked had a darker part of their lives outside of everyone's knowledge. Perhaps they were involved in something more nefarious than they led on to believe. She couldn't believe she was questioning those she relied on, but she didn't know who she could truly trust anymore. At this point in her life, was it really worth it to be involved in secret organizations and movements? Was that the point of her life, to cling to the shadows and strike like a serpent, always hiding and waiting for her prey to stumble and for herself to move in?

She had to believe that there was more to what she was doing than a petty quarrel with a political entity that didn't exist two or three hundred years ago. Empires rise and fall, that was the nature of things. She was fully aware of that, but what she stumbled upon there in front of her was something greater than cults and secret societies; it was a celestial playground that wanted to include her world in the mess its children made.

Kacyn placed a hand on her arm, as gentle as she'd always done, and smiled warmly. "It's the right decision, Majjai," she said calmly while no one else was paying attention. Ayela took a deep breath and copied the file onto her thumbdrive, and then shut the device down.

"We're ready," she declared, standing to her feet and quickly rushing over to her luggage. It took her no time to pack, and when she was done, everyone was waiting to leave.

"Let's move. We'll pick up new phones in Hes'Lierre on the way to Shamol. I have a contact waiting to pick us up at the edge of Cassum," Kamille said. Ayela took a deep breath and looked down at her thumbdrive, and then followed the others out of the room.

...What are you trying to tell me, Hashem?

Chapter 18

Southton was finally his again. Kudaj reveled in their victory. Their troops came in and had taken back what was stolen in just a couple of days, and their gains couldn't have been sweeter. The sensation was as pleasurable as strong alcohol or a good meal. They cheered, shouted, sang, and danced around campfires while they enjoyed fine foods their grateful citizens prepared for them, and parties with feasts were hosted in every town and city that was once laid under seize by the empire.

"Cheers to Prince Kudaj, Sovereign Liberator Apparent!" They shouted with raised mugs of ale, whiskey, and whatever other drinks the towns-folk brought them. Even the chirping insects and nighttime creatures seemed to celebrate with them. Music played from local practitioners, and stories were told by the soldiers to swoon whoever they'd set their sights on.

For Kudaj, though, he didn't care too much for romance. At least, he liked to believe that. His heart was sealed up, locked away until he saw the empire burn for taking from him what he longed for most; the company of his lost sister. A company he would never get the chance to enjoy in this life.

"Your Highness," said a certain soldier as she casually made her way over to him. She was beautiful, and a true Songrivan through-and-through. Her scarlet hair glistened in the moonlight and in the light of the campfire, and he wasn't too drunk to appreciate the silhouette of her figure against the fire behind her. She'd taken her armor off and settled into something more comfortable, as most of them did.

"Commander Jürdae," he responded gently.

Though shadow cloaked her face, he could sense the smile underneath. "You're not sitting with the others. I figured I'd check on you." She cooed softly. He could hear the worry in her voice, and it was justified. They'd been friends for many years, and she'd gotten to know him quite well. She also knew how the family-line of the Sovereign was preserved, and she was not of noble birth. She kept herself humble with the special privilege she was given with him, never asking too much or taking advantage of their close friendship. She always kept herself from flirting with him in any way.

...Until that night.

"There's much to contemplate, Jürdae. Even the whiskey is having a hard time getting through to me," he admitted. She took another step closer to him. He could almost make out her crimson eyes behind the shadows of the evening. He could smell her perfume, a curious thing for a soldier to bring with her to a warfront.

"That's a fascinating scent you wear," he said. She smirked.

"One of the town's girls let me wear a couple sprays. I figured it'd be nice to not smell like sweat and dirt at the end of the day while we're all celebrating," she said, getting a little closer to him. Perhaps he did have room for romance in his life. Perhaps he could open up a little more to someone who was already so close to him. Perhaps he didn't care about *family purity* and other nonsense that his father prided himself with. There was certainly a time for traditions to be broken, and why couldn't it have been him?

So he took his chance and tossed his family tradition to the wind. He forgot about the burning anger he held in his heart for a moment, the pain of losing his sister, and he embraced the comfort this woman seemed to offer him in that moment.

"It smells beautiful," he started, gentle sliding his hand to the small of her back. He could tell she was flustered and taken a bit by surprise, but he could also tell that she wanted his touch. His heart began to beat a little harder when he felt the sensation of her body pressed against his, only the cloth of their tunics separating their skin. "It's a fitting compliment to a woman so beautiful," he added.

"My prince," she stammered. Then, in a whisper into his ear, she said, "Are you sure this is what you want? Won't your family have something to say?"

He didn't answer her with a word, but with a kiss.

Passionate.

Longing.

Encapsulating.

He felt numb from pleasure, and he could tell she did too. "To Hell with what my family has to say, Jürdae," he said softly. She pulled away, but didn't let go of his hand as she led him away from the celebration. Far enough away, they embraced their romance with gentleness and passion, and drank deep of each other's love long into the night. As long as they were able, in the comfort of his personal tent, they carried a newfound desire and craving that intoxicated them with such heightened bliss...

And his dreams were filled with the sounds of her voice, as hers were with his...

VI

Episode 6

Farseer

Chapter 19

"Thank the makers we're out of that bloody car," Thillan exclaimed, stretching his arms high into the air and yawning. "I couldn't have been more couped up in it. How we managed to fit five bloody people *and* the driver is beyond me."

"Keep complaining and we'll put you in the trunk next time," Asher snickered as he tossed a bag at him and closed the rear. The car quickly sped off and lost itself in the moving traffic. The girls chuckled and slung their bags over their shoulders.

"Remind me why we're here again?" Ayela asked as they walked into the check-in office at the motel.

"To give ourselves a bit of a break. We've been on the road for a day and a half, and before that we were embarking on a dangerous mission and traveling all over thaerv without even a second to collect ourselves. We're just taking a break for a night, and then we'll be back on the road," he answered truthfully, much to Ayela's surprise. They were in such a public place, she was sure someone would raise an eyebrow at them.

"Ah, Asher. It's been a long while, friend," the dwarven clerk at the desk said as they approached. He was a shorter man, only a head taller than Ayela. His accent was thick, announcing his immigration from the City-States to their *glorious* empire. He was balding a little, and wore a thick, black beard. He had a little bit of a stomach, but it was complimented with thick arms and broad shoulders. One of his pointed ears was folded over, likely from an accident he'd gotten himself into.

"Too long, Kag'n. You heard the news?" Asher asked as the dwarf handed him a room key. Ayela assumed he'd been here many times before.

"Aye. Bad mess that one is. Only, I'm not so convinced those sods were truly Durinveii. No Governor from the States would send agents to attack another country like that, even if they *were* Zadist. The Lord-President does his best to maintain peace on all fronts, save for those sorry *blood elves* – no offense," he said, nodding over at Ayela. She glared at him, but didn't let it linger.

"I agree – about the States not attacking another country outright like they supposedly did here," Asher said, implying what they'd discovered. Even though Kag'n didn't betray it with his expression, she could tell he knew what Asher meant. "Anyways, we're just going to offload in our room and stay in town for the night. *Stick to the shadows, ye huddled foes.*"

"*And in the shadows, thy secrets be known.* Enjoy your stay, ya salty dog," Kag'n said with a smirk. Asher returned his smile and led them to their room.

The rest of the day was spent with the girls walking around the city while the boys paid a visit to the bar for a couple drinks. They enjoyed their time off, but Ayela had a bad feeling in the pit of her gut. It seemed like there was something at every turn, waiting to jump out of the shadows and attack her. Things were going too smoothly. Sure, they had their share of close calls, but things were ultimately going well, and that made Ayela paranoid.

As the three of them wandered down the street in the early evening hours, they spent their time sharing stories from their childhood and wandering into different stores to explore what they had for sale. Eventually, they ended up at a café, ordering coffee and enjoying the cool, easy night.

"Something feels off," Ayela said, interrupting their conversation about Kamille's entry into the darkling organization. "I'm sorry, I don't mean to be rude, but something just feels off."

"What do you mean?" Kamille asked, taking another sip of her coffee. They were fortunate enough that no one was sitting at any of the other wire tables outside with them, and any pedestrians were engrossed in their own conversations and activities to pay them any mind.

"You don't think it's weird how well any of this has gone? Like, no one has suspected our activities at all since we've embarked on this mission... No one has detected us, no one has listened in... Something just feels off," Ayela remarked.

Kacyn sighed, and it felt as though Ayela's heart dropped into her stomach. "...I haven't been completely honest with you," she began. Before she had the chance to continue, though, dark clouds began to form overhead, blocking out what little sunlight remained in the twilight hours. The wind suddenly started to pick up, and a roll of thunder ominously vibrated the ground from overhead. They girls stood to her feet, and Ayela started to sense that dark presence Kacyn felt in D'Vnora.

Then, like a ghost coming to haunt her from her deepest and darkest nightmares, a smooth and seductive voice called out from behind her. Kamille's eyes widened, and Kacyn's expression fell with fear. It was a voice that made Ayela's skin crawl, reminding her that the one who took Rhaja's life was still out alive and active...

...And then Tallie said, "Hello, *dancer...*"

Chapter 20

The winds were stronger with each passing second, but not strong enough to knock the imperial warships out of the air. Spotlights shown all around, and there was an announcement for civilians to stay in their homes. For Kamille, Kacyn, and Ayela, though, they stood face-to-face with the darkest witch ever born: Tallie.

Her golden locks were tied into a finely brushed ponytail behind her head that fell to the middle of her back, and she wore a black coat that extended past her knees. Black leather boots were strapped up to her thighs, and Ayela could make out her lacy black top underneath her coat. Nothing compared, though, to the wickedness contained in those sapphire gems that served as her eyes.

"What are you doing here, Talle," Ayela spat. Instinctively, she had already tapped into her reserves of divine logic. Imperial warships hovered overhead, amplifying the imposed martial law, and the storms raged harder with every passing second.

Had she called forth an aethril?

"I'm actually here for her, young blood elf," Tallie said with a sly grin. "Did she tell you anything about herself?"

Kamille scoffed at the witch. "She doesn't need to. Kacyn, are you turning us in to the Kult?"

Kacyn shook her head wildly. "Never," she declared.

"Then there you have it, ivory *bitch*. She's on our side regardless of whether her stories about herself are true or not," Kamille answered. Talle laughed maniacally.

"You truly have no idea! This is rich!" She spat. Ayela could almost feel her blood boil with anger. "This girl is Songrivan, as I'm sure she's no doubt told you: but she's been with the Kult as long as she can remember! She ran away a year before our encounter, mighty dancer, but she was *so* determined to find you when she heard that a dancer existed outside of the royal family of the Sovereignty, that she *actually* came back to Enthedrill! It's too funny!"

Ayela was shocked at this sudden revelation. "Is this true?" She asked, slowly looking over at the Ebony elf. Tears flooded down Kacyn's cheeks, and she could see the remorse and hatred in her eyes; she *hated* the Kult. She hated them as much as Ayela did, if not more.

"They took *everything* from me!" She sobbed in anger and sadness. "They stole me from my parents when I was a baby... Her people were told by her demon-gods that I was a farseer, and then they raised me like I was a caged animal! I was always chained, always beaten, always *starved!* They lied, they stole, they destroyed... I never got the chance to have friends or see people my age, because whenever I did make friends, they *killed* them all! They're monsters!"

Neither Ayela nor Kamille could blame Kacyn for lying about her past. Why would anyone want to admit ties to such a horrible order like the one Tallie belonged to? "I'm so sorry, Emira," Ayela cooed. Kacyn buried her hands in her face and cried like an abandoned child. Then the dancer's eyes turned to Tallie, and the same wrath she felt when she realized that it was *her* that killed Rhaja resurfaced. "You're going to *pay* for all the things you've done!"

"Am I? You darklings can't kill... And you see, there were many infants stolen from all over the world, deary... You think Kacyn is the only one? Grow up! This is the way of the world!" Tallie spat before reaching for the sky. When her arm was extended fully, violet runes and circles etched themselves out of thin air, illuminating the space they hovered around her arm as a stream of purple energy spewed forth into the clouds above.

Then, a massive rune was carved into the storm, and before they knew it, the winds raged as hard as they did the night Sümol was attacked. Ayela's eyes widened; she knew exactly what was happening...

...Tallie was summoning an aethril from the storms overhead.

"Get the men out here, she's calling down a god!" Ayela shouted over the wrathful storm.

"Are you crazy?! What the *fuck* are you going to do?!" Kamille shouted. Kacyn approached both of them with her arm over her face as if to block the winds. One wrong move, and they could be swept up into the maelstrom that hovered overhead.

"I can see aethrils!" She shouted. Ayela and Kamille looked at her as if she'd lost her mind.

"We can all bloody see them, Kacyn!"

"No, I mean I can *see* them! I know what they look like and where to strike them! That's one of the reasons Tallie wants me so badly! I can see clearly what beings of higher dimensions look like!" She clarified. They looked even more confused, but Ayela understood what she was saying.

"You go, get the guys! Kacyn and I will fight Tallie and her pet god!" She ordered.

"But-"

"These people in this town are counting on you

fighting back the empire! Go!"

Kamille wasn't given a chance to protest. Ayela and Kacyn turned to face Tallie, who was laughing hysterically. Kamille ran like Hell for the bar they were staying at, careful to avoid the troops that were dropping all around from the dropships that descended from the massive carriers hovering above.

"I'm with you, Majjai!" Kacyn declared. Ayela assumed her most favored martial artist's stance, and they readied themselves to fight the Towlålite witch.

Time seemed to slow down as Tallie levitated off the ground. Her wicked smile never left her face, and as she held her hands out, orbs of purple light hovered above her palms while ethereal ribbons of light glowing the same color circle around her body. This was going to be her hardest fight, but Ayela knew that this was what she was meant for. Fighting off the Towlålites was her calling. They posed a threat to her world, and she would fight dearly to protect it.

"You think you stand a chance against the might of the gods of old?!" She shouted.

"No," Ayela retorted above the deafening winds. "Not alone, at least..."

"...But together, Emira and I can do the impossible!"

Chapter 21

The grounds shook.

The thunder clapped violently.

The lightning flashed with each blue peal.

In front of each bolt, ominously towering over the homes, apartments and stores was an aethril she was all too familiar with. The winds raged with the fury of a chained god, and Tallie's twisted laughter could be heard over the chaos and the noise that threatened to throw Ayela and Kacyn like dolls.

"It's *him!*" Kacyn yelled, gripping Ayela's hand with an iron hold. "It's *Lukrinael,* the high god of the Yglsora! She's managed to chain the strongest of the old ones!"

The name alone was enough to inspire fear. Nothing she believed about the Kult in the past mattered; Tallie subdued the mightiest servant of Rök that her religion had ever named. All that mattered was that he be released from his imprisonment to the witch.

"You can see him clearly?!" She shouted back.

Kacyn's eyes began to glow, and she could *feel*

the power emulating from the Ebony elf. She could see why the Kult wanted her as badly as they do; she was *powerful*. "Yes!" She answered. "But this won't be easy!"

Before either had the chance to respond, Kacyn shoved her out of the way. A blast of purple energy ripped by them, promising to strike Ayela's head. She got up and readied herself as Tallie stomped towards her. The aethril wasted no time in summoning bright, cyan-colored runes out of the clouds that poured beams of energy and destruction down onto the town. Explosions rocked the ground beneath, knocking all but Tallie over, and the soldiers that were detached began to open fire in the distance. It was clear now; they were there to execute their own people.

Ayela's heart burned with pure, focused rage. Her vision began to change hues, giving everything a reddish tint as she stood to her feet. Her hair whipped wildly in the wind, and though the rain soaked her clothes, she felt her body temperature rise from her anger. *Not again!* She thought to herself.

"I WON'T FUCKING LET YOU SLAUGHTER THESE PEOPLE!!!"

The world fell silent around her save for her own

heavy breaths and stomping feet as she charged forward. She couldn't even hear Kacyn as she cheered her on. All she could hear and see was the twisted laughter of her heartless enemy, and the face of the one who murdered her lover in cold blood because... All because of a prophecy.

When she was close enough, she leapt into the air. She tapped into the deepest parts of her heart, and hurled a telekinetic blast so powerful, it punched a crater into the ground where Tallie stood. The witch was fast, though, and dodged the attack just in time. Then the battle ensued.

It was a duel of the logicians.

A battle against the dark and the divine.

It was a fight long overdue, and an exactment of revenge that Ayela had forgotten she craved. There was chaos as everyone fought, and while the dancer and the dark mage tossed blasts of their respective magics at each other, Kacyn looked around her environment with dread and confusion. The leader of the revival she longed for had given in to her darkest desires, and the highest god of her ancient order was bringing death and destruction to a people long oppressed by the very empire opening fire on them.

Her vision was active, and she was an open channel to the divine logic she long held access to. A continuous flow of strange, eldritch energy coursed through her from the divine that existed beyond reality, and she suddenly became aware of the supernatural energies that everyone around her held.

Kacyn could feel it all.

The soldiers who were husks of blind obedience.

The citizens that were husks of blind obstinance.

The mages that were agents of blind devotion.

She looked up at the god Tallie had summoned, seeing it more clearly than anyone ever had. In her vision, there was no darkness. Everything was equally illuminated, and she could see all as if the sun were out on a clear day. The clouds above were roiling masses of steam and vapor collected together like a smokescreen or a veil between their reality and the reality beyond.

And there, behind the clouds, she saw *him*. She saw Lukrinael as if the clouds weren't even there, a being that glowed like a bright star being eclipsed. His body was strange even to her mind's eye; a blue torso carried by strong legs, with four massive arms hovering around the shoulders as if they were attached - but they weren't. His head hovered above the shoulders where the neck ought to be, and his face was ethereal and strange; emotionless, frozen in the same blank expression the statue of a god would have.

Nothing was still, either. She stared at him in awe

and amazement, watching as his skin rippled like it were the surface of a body of water, but the ripples were only like an image that echoed across his skin with each step. His face was the same way, but even more than that, it looked like his face would twist in halves, spinning outward onto itself, and giving way for a new face to take its place.

When she looked at him, though, she saw the deepest parts of his being and an emotion that she herself felt all-too familiar with; despair. He was captured and subject to the authority of a dark witch through the acts of dark and binding magic. It was an eldritch spell that bound an eldritch god, and the emotion he felt was something that resonated deeply in her core.

Free him.

A voice louder than the storms around but quieter than a whisper spoke into her mind's ear. A nameless voice, disembodied and hidden from the conscious or subconscious eye. She looked around to see if some specter had snuck up behind her, but there was no one... And yet, she *knew* who it was that spoke to her.

Hashem.

The divine one of Ayela's faith, the highest of all divine beings. The one not bound to religion or rules like the other gods were. The one who created the gods and put them in their place, the horrifying and awesome one that blessed her with the vision she now used. The Name, hidden to all, was the one who commanded Lukrinael's freedom.

But how? She wasn't a dancer. She wasn't able to attack with her powers, or bind and unbind anything with them. All she could do was *see.* Perhaps that was the point, though; she could see what no one else could. The dancer wasn't able to see, but she could control the fabrics of reality that Kacyn *could* see. She looked up at Lukrinael once more, who slowly looked over at her with a familiar sadness in his eyes – and then she saw it.

Around his wrists were golden braces to match the belt and waistcloth he wore, and around his ankles were ethereal shackles that stretched through matter and reality until they connected to Tallie's heart. It was spiritual, ethereal; she bound the god to herself, using dark magic to keep it enslaved to her will. If they cut off the god's ankles and wrists, they would free him to return to the heavens where he resided and could heal. He would no longer be bound to a witch of thaerv.

But how?

...How could she reach a woman so scorned?

Chapter 22

Ayela fought hard, throwing everything she had at Tallie. The witch didn't back down or make it easy, but the dancer wasn't tired in the slightest. Every so often, her adversary would unleash a barrage of violet blasts that matched the color of Ayela's eyes, but she would defend herself with a shield of invisible energy.

She maintained a continued stream of routines and martial artist's moves that flowed perfectly into each other, flexing the entirety of her life's training as she fought against the leader of the Towlåalites, but she was matched in every way. It was fitting; the new leader of the Tribes head-to-head against the leader of the Kult. It was a test of might, a duel of light and dark to see who would forever remain victorious.

But in their fighting, Ayela had lost herself to her bitter rage. Every wound reopened. Every painful memory came to the surface, and vengeance drove her actions rather than a heart of justice and mercy.

She was out for blood, and each wild toss and kick she made was a testimony of her bloodlust.

"You fancy yourself a hero, Aylea? Your kind terrorized my people throughout *all* of thaerv's history!" Tallie shouted above the winds. They paused their fighting to catch their breaths. The fires from the destroyed buildings all around kept their battlefield illuminated, and Ayela was too enraged to notice the soldiers fighting some unseen force off in the distance. The ships above remained perfectly in place, as if to oversee the battles below and ensure everything went in their favor, and Kacyn stood to her feet, yelling something at her that she couldn't understand. It wasn't because she couldn't hear the farseer, though; it was because she was too angry to listen.

"Your order terrorized the *world!* There isn't a catastrophe in history that doesn't have your people's involvement, Tallie! Death and destruction is *all that you've wrought* on remankind!" Ayela barked. "You want to preach about being the hero?! You killed an entire town because of superstition! You enslaved a god because of a hunger for power! It's like you people can't get enough!"

"You don't understand, *blood elf!*"

"Stop *fucking* calling me that!" Ayela screamed. She threw her hand out in anger and clenched her fist, and Tallie's body tightened up as if ropes had wrapped around her. She yelped and grunted as she struggled to break free, but the more she struggled, the tighter Ayela's ethereal grip clenched. Her fist began to shake with how hard she squeezed, and then Tallie started to levitate off the ground.

"Ayela, NO!!!" Kacyn panicked.

Tallie shrieked from the pain, and it only pushed Ayela to crush her harder and harder. She could hear the cracking sounds above the winds. "I. Will. Make. You. PAY!!!" She growled.

"AYELA!!!" Kacyn shrieked before tackling into the red-haired Songrivan. Tallie dropped to the ground and coughed up blood. As the ivory witch tried to stand up, though, she grunted and fell back to her knees, clenching her side as she coughed up more blood. If Kacyn hadn't stopped her, Ayela would have broken more than her ribs. "This is not our way!"

"But she took *everything* from me! She took my Rhaja, she took my gods, my religion... She stole everything from me!" Ayela shouted as she stood to her feet. She marched over to the Towlålite and lifted a palm into the air with every one of her muscles tensed. Tallie cried in pain as she was suspended into the air, and then Ayela saw it...

The *fear* in Tallie's eyes.

For once in her life, someone was *terrified* of Ayela. Someone feared her power. She suddenly became exactly what the empire said she was. She became aware of the town's destruction around her, and worried for her friends' safety. Rage had consumed her and turned her into something she was not, and an entire town of people could have been saved when they weren't. The soldiers continued to fire at something in the distance, and it gave her hope that not everything was lost.

"I'm sorry," she whispered, gently setting Tallie on the ground.

Before she could do anything else, though, Kacyn placed a hand on her shoulder. "I know how to stop the aethril!" She yelled over the winds. She turned and looked up at the black clouds and stared into the glowing eyes that once stood over her wrecked home in Sümol.

"Let's take down a god..."

VII

Episode 7

Fragility

Chapter 23

Soldiers opened fire, firmly standing their ground against the raging storm of the aethril, covering each other when they needed to reload. They hoped that they would eventually wear down the cover that the destruction provided for Thillan, Asher and Kamille. The three of them crouched behind fallen debris, holding rifles from unfortunate soldiers that were in the way of the destruction, and surrounded by other citizens that had picked up weapons and joined them in the fight. They only shot at knees, arms, and anywhere else that wouldn't lead to death, but the citizens that fought beside them didn't care whether the enemy lived or died.

They were bitter, and rightfully so.

"Keep pushing!" Asher shouted as they peaked around the debris and continued to open fire. There were women and children hiding farther back, but there were still more citizens that weren't dead, trapped in the buildings behind the enemy line. They needed to fight for them. They needed to get as many survivors as possible. They needed to tell the people how the empire descended down upon them when the aethrils attacked, and offered them up like sacrifices.

In that moment, the three of them were the heroes they fought their whole lives to be. They pushed back the empire, showed that the tyrants *could* be beaten. They showed that the ones who stuck to oppressive traditions didn't have the power they thought they did, and that skin colors and statuses didn't determine who got to be the good ones in this historic moment.

Kamille knew that Ayela was giving *that witch* absolute hell, and she didn't care if Tallie made it out alive or not – she just hoped that they kicked her ass to the deepest pits of hell that she belonged in. In that moment, they were the ones fighting for the people.

"Let's get them!" She screamed, standing to her feet and opening fire. The shouts of the others joined her voice, and their line erupted in gunfire against the soldiers, taking them out in rows. Their confidence was boosted, and they emerged from behind their cover. They pushed forward, filling the skies with thunderous war cries louder than the storm could ever hope to match, and when the soldiers stopped shooting and started running, they charged after them in the heat of emotion and newfound energy.

The three of them were there in the front, leading the charge and showing that the darklings weren't afraid to get their hands dirty once in a while. It was a scene to be told in the epics of history, and Kamille told herself she would never back down from an oppressor or a fight ever again if they survived that moment. She would let this victory fuel her...

...When she led a charge that sent the empire running for their lives.

Chapter 24

There they stood, dancer and farseer, facing off against a god chained to the choking, bleeding witch that laid on the ground behind them. Tallie was no longer a threat, too damaged to get up and fight with them anymore. The only thing they needed to do now was sever the bond between her and Lukrinael.

Amidst her wheezing, Tallie managed to maintain her maniacal laughter. "You can't stop him, nor can you stop us," she coughed. "You asked why I and my people believe the way we do? Why we were behind every catastrophe known to elvish history? It's because of *your* god, Ayela. You're Rök. He created a universe damned, and many more beyond it. And us... We were subjected to its horrors! Don't you see? My gods want to free this universe from his cursed grasp! We want to be free, no longer told that we're imperfections! And we will stop at nothing to take what's ours away from him!"

"Majjai, ignore her! Don't listen to her! She's

manipulated by the Towlål!"

"Yes, *Majjai* – oh leader of the new Tribes of Enthedrill – don't listen to me! Listen to the god you hope to free! What do you think he'll do once he *is* free?! He'll want revenge!" Tallie spat. Ayela looked on at the glowing eyes, and for a moment, she thought she saw sadness in their bright illumination.

Free him.

A voice whispered into her mind, familiar and ancient, loud but silent. A voice that carried the humility of one unafraid to admit their mistakes, but also as ancient and powerful as the god she believed in. It had to be. It must have been Hashem. It was the only way her god spoke to her – a gentle whisper behind her mind, reassuring her and comforting her.

"I don't trust you," Ayela declared.

"I know you don't, but you don't have to," Tallie continued. "The world will fall under the control the Order, and then the universe will fall, the universes beyond, and then all the Blind Eternities in between all universes will be subject to the will of the Towlål!"

Then Kacyn faced her with clenched fists. "You understand nothing! Don't you see?! The Towlål aren't the gods you think they are! They *can't* conquer the Blind Eternities any more than they can conquer Rök!" She yelled. "The Blind Eternities *are* Rök!"

Ayela knew what they were talking about, but she just couldn't wrap her mind around it. The Blind Eternities were the heavens that Rök and the gods all dwelt in, but with Kacyn's declaration, she no longer knew what to believe. Was it true? Was her god the all-encompassing heavens that reached to the horizons of infinity? The revelation was so profound to Tallie, though, that she could see the despair and distress wash over her like water.

"You're wrong!" She cried. "You're wrong! I devoted my *life* to the Order – no, to the Towlål! You're lying to me!"

"Ask the god you bound! Ask one who can't lie!"

They faced the god altogether, who watched them in amusement.

"The irony, mighty witch, is that you believe your dark gods ever cared about the dealings of mortals like the aethril do."

His declaration given with a voice of thunder shattered Tallie's entire world, and they could see it all over her face. She coughed as she tried to stand up, but could only manage to get up to her hands and knees.

Then, at her lowest point, she let out a heart-shattering wail, as if she'd lost everything she'd worked her entire life to get. Ayela began to pity her, and looked away as the witch sobbed and cried harder than she'd ever heard anyone cry before. She knew why, though; Tallie's entire life had been a lie. Everything she did, all she accomplished, the dark order she supported – it was all for a lie.

Kacyn placed a hand on her shoulder, pulling her from her thoughts. "Tallie was like me... Her childhood was taken from her by her parents. She comes from a long line of warlocks, and just like them, she was indoctrinated and raised in the Kult since she could walk."

"...I want to have empathy for her... I want to forgive her... But I can't forget what she's done..." Ayela said.

"So don't forget."

The words pierced through Ayela's heart like an arrow. "You don't have to forget to forgive. That's not the point. You just need to let it go. That's how you show her you're different," Kacyn said. Ayela took a deep breath and let her own tears fall, then turned towards the aethril once more. "I can show you where to strike."

She gripped Ayela's shoulder firmly, and suddenly her vision changed. No longer was there darkness or illusions. She could clearly see the clouds of the storm, twirling around on themselves. She could see the aura and energy surrounding each of them, highlighting them in clouds of color. Most of all, though, she could see the aethril as clear as she could see everyone else.

It was a haunting image that would stay with her the rest of her life.

"Just above the shackles on his wrists and ankles. Now. While you have the chance. While the witch is grieving," Kacyn urged.

She obeyed, picturing in her mind blades of invisible energy, sharp enough to cut through any material. She pulled from her memories the most graceful of dance routines she'd learned from her own people, and she reached from the deepest parts of her inner being to fuel her divine logic. In her final spin, she flung the energy at the god with a pained cry. She watched as the telekinetic blades, now visible, like cleavers made of the smoothest glass that soared towards his limbs that he held out like an ancient slave ready to be free of his bonds. The god cried thunderously in pain as his hands and feet were severed, and as he began to dissipate into nothingness, he smiled and said, "thank you, logicians." Lukrinael was free at last.

The storm began to vanish, and the fires slowly fizzled out from the destruction they wrought. Soldiers began to flee from the wreckage, while their pursuers – the townsfolk led by Thillan, Asher, and Kamille herself – chased them back to their drop ships. Ayela and Kacyn reveled in a sweet victory they were not expecting to achieve.

A victory that was darkened by the angry cries of a scorned witch...

Chapter 25

"*You!* You two destroyed *everything* I've dedicated my life to!" Tallie growled as she struggled to her feet. Tears still streaked down her dirt-stained face. She clenched her ribs from the intense pain she felt as she tried to march towards them. They both backed away further with each step she took. "You have *no idea* what will happen to thaerv if I don't promise a sacrifice to the Towlål! And you stole away my only *defense* against them! You ruined *everything!*"

"Ma'am! We need to get you out of here!" One of the commanders yelled as a detachment approached from behind the wreckage. Their rifles were trained on the logicians. Tallie continued to sob as she glared at them, as if she were contemplating how she would kill them where they stood. "Ma'am!"

"We can end this now, Tallie," Ayela started. "Just walk away. Leave with your detachment. Leave with your empire. Continue trying to control the world, so that we can continue trying to stop you... If you try anything now, I will put you down permanently."

Tallie kept glaring at them, but after a few minutes of contemplation, she turned as if she were going to leave. Kacyn and Ayela were relaxed for a moment...

...Just long enough for the witch to etch a spell out of their notice.

A long pike of violet energy shot forth from her hand, aimed at Ayela's heart with speed enough that it should have landed the hit. What Tallie didn't anticipate, though, was Kacyn's instinct to protect her friends at all costs. Her strange, confusing foresight was a gift in many ways, but in that moment, it would prove to be a fatal curse.

She shoved Ayela out of the way, and time seemed to move slowly as she watched the spear of magic painfully pierce through Kacyn's chest. The clear sky would have been better served with clouds as the crimson morning sun began to peek over the horizon, for Ayela's heart would drown in sorrow like how the town should have drowned in the deepest of rainfall.

All sound was muffled, and her body was numb from shock as she watched Kacyn fall to the ground with scarlet blood pouring forth in a puddle on the road beneath. She couldn't hear the soldiers as they dragged Tallie back to their dropship. She couldn't hear herself when she yelled out Kacyn's name, nor could she hear her friends when they shouted and cried at the Ebony elf lying on the ground, coughing up blood.

"No, no, no, no!" She sobbed, rushing over to her fallen friend as quickly as she could.

"It's...Okay," Kacyn managed. "This is the way of things...Isn't it?"

Ayela couldn't hold back her tears. "You-"

"Couldn't let you die, Majjai... I couldn't let you die... Not by *her* hands..."

The others made it over as quickly as they could, and crouched down beside the two of them. Those of the town who survived the attack formed a somber circle around them, while the ships of the empire soared off into the sunrise.

"...Emira," Ayela cried. "Thank you for everything you did..."

Kacyn smiled and held her face. "I hope...The gods saw what you did here, Majjai..." She said as she took her final breath. Ayela watched with pain as the life left her eyes. Her pupils dialated, and her lungs exhaled any air left in them. Her hand was about to fall, but Ayela caught it in time and held it to her lips. And then she clenched fistfuls of her shirt and wept. Tears fell onto her lifeless face...

...Ayela wished she'd never let Tallie live.

Chapter 26

The townsfolk spent the day with them, clearing a space for all the dead and fallen that they could find. They dug the graves as quickly as they could. So many that were placed in the ground, that there was at least one person that knew each of those who lost their lives, and Kacyn was laid in the center of the graveyard as their fallen hero. A hero who gave her life for the sake of the many. Another divine logician to inspire hope.

As the evening began to set, they covered the bodies and lit torches at the heads of each grave, and they gathered around the burial site with somber and solemn expressions. As they looked on, many wept and mourned the fallen. Parents mourned for their young children that were caught in the wreckages. Husbands and wives mourned for their partners caught in the firing line of the invading soldiers. Seeds of doubt and pain were sown...

...Seeds of rebellion were planted and watered by

the tears of betrayal.

"Everyone," Asher shouted, demanding everyone's attention, "this is what our empire has become. A lawless, boundless, immoral group of bullies that use their power for experiments and dealings with beings they don't understand! They hoard our wealth, slaughter our people, and perpetuate lies about what we are supposed to look like *and* act like!"

Some of the people shouted in affirmation and raised their fists. They were angry, distraught, and wounded that they were treated so poorly. "They were afraid that the divine logicians have returned, and they had *every right* to be afraid! The hero among the fallen... Emira... She helped Majjai fight an *aethril!* Imagine what her legacy would mean if the survivors of an attack they launched – people they *weren't expecting to live* – show up at the doorstep of the emperor himself and demand he answer for his crimes?!"

"Yeah!" One of the men called out.

"That's what I mean! Keep that fire going! You all just survived an *aethril attack!* No one has ever done that so far! No one has survived! No one... Until now! Carry this fire, friends, and use it to set the entire empire ablaze!" He continued.

Then Ayela stepped forward, and all eyes were

on her. Her face was downcast, and she nervously brushed off the black lace dress she wore to the funeral. "...They were our friends and our families," she began, tears falling from her cheeks. She knew that she didn't know anyone besides Kacyn, but they were all feeling the pain she felt in her heart. "And the empire would have their deaths mean nothing... We owe it to them to make sure that doesn't happen."

"That's right!"

"Speak, Majjai!"

"We will never forget!"

She took a deep breath, and roiled all of her anxious tension. This was bigger than the darklings. Bigger than the wars they'd discovered. The empire declared an attack on its own people by slaughtering the innocent. They encouraged war with their own citizens by unleashing a chained god on them, and they would learn why that was such a mistake.

"We owe it to the fallen from this town, and every place they attacked before this one! For Sümol! For the divine logician they claimed to have killed before! To every one of my kind they hunted down and slaughtered like animals! We owe it to them to take this stand here and now!"

The proclamation did little to lift the heavy burden of their spirits, but it did feed the flame burning in their hearts. She wasn't sure how she could continue forward herself, though. Kamille seemed to sense that, and placed a hand on her shoulder. She looked to the ground, and watched the droplets fall from her face to the dirt beneath. Why did the empire do this? Why did people of power align themselves with such horrible and wretched organizations? Was it the promise of power and security that drove them to treat the ones on the bottom with such disregard and contempt? Her heart was shattered to pieces, but most of all...

...She realized how broken everything else in her life was.

VIII

Episode 8

Climbing

Chapter 27

"Your highness!" Called a soldier as he entered the planning room. Kudaj stood around a table with a map of Songriveii illuminated in the center. Holographic projections of Songrivan soldiers were placed in various strategic locations across the Easton regions. The prince was planning his next moves against the empire. "We've received an important message from the Lord-President of Durinveii! The empire invades!"

"Bloody *fucking* fools!" Kudaj spat with a smirk. "The Emperor truly doesn't know the mess he walks into... If he assumes he can simply walk up on the shores of the Songrivans *and* the dwarves, he's a bigger idiot than I ever gave him credit for."

"They're requesting an audience with the Sovereign and his prince, your highness. Shall I set up a call?"

"Yes. Set the meeting time for a half-hour from now," Kudaj ordered.

"Yes, your highness!"

The others in the room had grins as wide as the prince's after the soldier left the chamber. He reveled in their soon-forged allegiance to the States, eager to combine their efforts and reclaim their lands. He folded his arms across his chest and took a deep breath, hoping for only the brightest of futures for all nations and peoples of thaerv. All elves would be free of imperial threat once and for all.

"This is a day long awaited, your highness," One of the generals said.

"Indeed. I can't deny that. We have longed for the day that the States cease their petty quarrel with us and join us against our enemies. This... This is going to be a day to go down in the history books. It's exactly like the Hadaj'Imad proclaimed on the day of my birth; *The world above and the world below will join together, as the heir of the crimson sun defeats the lord of the fallen east.* We are seeing this prophecy unfold, by the lips of our highest farseer," Kudaj declared. The generals snickered and nodded, no doubt encouraged by the remembrance of the High Farseer of Centerton.

"Shall we contemplate our next plan of action while we wait?" Another of the generals asked.

He paused for a moment. "Yes. Let's plan," he started. His mind went to Jürdae, a woman he'd discovered his true feelings for. He longed for a public relationship with her, and as he contemplated their next course of action, he concocted a way that just might make it happen. It was so wild and imaginative, and it shouldn't work, but he was so confident in her ability and the undiscovered divine logic she wielded, that it *had* to work. So he planned, and none of his generals were the wiser of his true intentions.

The time had come. The generals were excused from their war meeting, and he was left in the room by himself. In front of him, the hologram of Songriveii remained, but after a few seconds, another image of his father appeared. Tall, broad, and even though his long hair and braided beard were greying, he still looked full of vigor and energy. He was dressed in his royal armor; a golden breastplate, pauldrons that held his hood and cape which drooped to the floor into a majestic pile around his plated feet. A humble crown rested upon his head, signifying the mark of a Sovereign who earned his title through honest means.

"My son," he said, his voice deep and rumbling, like rolls of thunder in a mighty storm. Even through hologram it carried its same weight. "How fares the warfront?"

"We have reclaimed Southton, reestablished the towns and villages that were attacked, and have begun planning our invasion into Easton," he declared proudly.

"Good work. You carry your mother's courage and boldness. Remember the teachings of Agabesh. Our gods will not fail you in this war," he encouraged. Kudaj smiled.

"I have not forgotten, Lord-Sovereign."

"I know, my son."

A flicker caught their attention, then the Lord-President of Durinveii appeared on the opposite from the Sovereign. He was as tall as Kudaj's father, just as broad, and just as proud. He wore a slick suit-and-tie. The President's skin was darker than most dwarves, and his hair seemed to be greying a bit as well, but he carried the same energy as his father.

"Sovereign," he said with a thick Durinveii accent.

"Lord-President," his father returned.

"I am pleased to meet with you both in these dark times. I know that the empire continues to invade your sacred shores. He has treated my lands with the same contempt," he began. "This audience you have so graciously offered me is to broker an alliance and cease-fire between our nations, that we might unify against the empire and bring an end to his reign, and if we need to, also divide the empire in a peace treaty. I am willing to overlook the theft of our most sacred gem so that we can overcome this enemy together."

"Pious, ignorant-"

"Father, please," Kudaj interrupted. There had been a strong tension between Durinveii and Songriveii for many years over a gem that both nations hold sacred. In both nation's history, they believed the gem to be a gift from the gods that grant its holder immense wealth and stability for their country. Throughout history, both countries had a habit of stealing it from each other, claiming it was theirs to begin with, and have feuded with each other since.

Kudaj cleared his throat and continued. "We will accept this forgiveness and willingly charter an alliance with you until this war is over with. But first, you and my father must set aside your prejudice and be willing to work together. This petty dispute over a bloody rock will cost us dearly if we cannot learn to coexist... Traditions serve us nothing if they do not aid in stopping a vicious enemy."

They were both silent for a few minutes, contemplating his words. "Your son is a wise man beyond his years, mighty Sovereign. You should be proud," the President said, breaking the silence.

"I am... Very well, Lord-President Solacian; we will broker an alliance until this war is over."

"Very good. I certainly hope that this strengthens

our relations from here on."

"My hope as well. Farewell," his father said. Then, Solacian's image vanished. He turned to Kudaj and offered a proud grin. "My amazement with your wisdom and ability to keep peace between adversaries continues to be a constant expression of mine, my son. Your mother is as proud as I am."

"Thank you, father."

"You are most welcome. When you're finished with the war planning, I require your presence in Centerton. We have more of your favorite things to deal with; beaurocracy and politics. The southern nobles are trying to cause a rift again."

Kudaj rolled his eyes. "Can't we replace them?"

"Ha! I only wish. Their people trust in their lies, so removing them would cause a total uprising. No, we must let them remain, and if their heir proves to be a secure successor that doesn't try to pull Southton away from the Sovereignty, they will not have charges brought against them."

"You're too gracious to worms like them," Kudaj said with a snicker. "I will return as soon as I can. May the gods guide your steps, father."

"And yours as well."

His father's image dissipated, and he was left in the room alone with his thoughts. Strange times were coming when Songriveii and their rivals would join together. He took a deep breath and waved his hand at the map of his nation, causing it to vanish into thin air. The lights came on as a response to the holograms disappearing. There was work to do, and though it didn't seem like it, he felt that the end of the war was in sight.

Soon, they would meet an era of peace...

Chapter 28

"Today marks the start of a new warfront as troops set down on the shores of Durinveii. In response to the attack on our cities and their people, the Emperor issued a statement regarding a retaliation, and today he has made good on his promises. Many mixed responses were generated from the people, as the residents of Vör and Esh make their support well known in interviews and surveys. The citizens of D'Vnora, Shustur, and even Laviport, however, protest against the war efforts, claiming that inequalities and climbing homelessness and unemployment statistics need the money more than the military institutions. What do you think, Koz-"

Kamille turned off the television and tossed the remote onto the table. They made it to Shamol safe and sound. The residents that they left behind promised to take their spark of rebellion and foster its growth. Emotions were still heavy, and though they'd only known each other for such a short period of time, Kacyn managed to sneak her way into Ayela's heart so powerfully, she hadn't realized how so until the farseer was no longer with them. They were going to forge a return for the Uri'Kai in a new way, and make a positive return and impact for the nation and the world. She was a beacon of mistreated light, stolen by the very people who wished to use her powers for destructive ends, and extinguish her when her uses were done...

...Like Tallie, in many ways.

"This isn't the way to honor her memory," Asher said with a firm tone of voice. He took another sip of his whiskey and set the glass down. The setting sun gave its last light through the blinders on the window. "So we failed to stop the war from happening, and we failed to stop an aethril. Kacyn gave her life for the very thing we risked ours for — and so much more. She wanted to bring the divine logicians back to the public in a powerful way. For us to just... To just sit here and mope around like we're failures is *not* how we honor her memory and death."

Ayela's ears perked, and she looked up at their leader. They'd heard the names she and Kacyn called each other, and on their journey back to Shamol, she explained their plans to them. She explained that they were going to see a return of the Uri'Kaii in a new form.

"Look at what her company helped us accomplish; breaking into one of the most secure vaults in the nation, discovering the truth behind a rotten war, and *even helping us take down a god.* Ayela, she helped you beat a god... A woman like her deserves our very best efforts in honor of her memory..."

Asher set the devices with all the downloaded secrets onto the table. They were still there, still preserved through everything. All of her memories of their adventures, all of them happening so quickly, filling their days with such excitement; they all raced through her mind like a film. How could she just give up? How could they sit and act like nothing ever happened, or sulk in their grieving misery like they all didn't go through Hell to get that information? Their plan wasn't a failure; it was just altered. And now there was one of their own who paid for those secrets with blood. They *needed* to continue their mission.

"So how do we get into the capital? I mean, that's a massive mesa it sits atop of, and it seems like the only way in our out of the city is through airship," Ayela asked.

Thillan nodded. Kamille chugged the rest of her ale before dropping her mug onto the table. "We spent three days here sulking while the empire is getting away with a war on Durinveii. Them and Songriveii need all the help they can get. So I agree; let's find a way into the capital. You asked how, love? It's simple; we need to climb the mesa and enter through the sewer tunnels that dump their waters into the air. If we use airships, we'll have to register. The moment they see the leaks, they'll go straight for us among any others that just flew in," she said.

"Climbing is going to be dangerous. We have to watch out for the hawks, and we need to make sure we have a plan for when we get into the city. Also, we can't spend too much time in the sewers. Kol'Ghouls and the Kikirat disease are still an issue," Asher explained.

Thillan cleared his throat before he began to speak. "There's a lot that needs to go into this, and we're gonna need to take a few weeks before actually releasing the leaks if we want to throw their scent off of us. One or two of you should live in the city, and someone needs to stay here to be a point of contact... We'll be setting up a cell in the Capital... "

"Agreed. Ayela and I can stay in the city. We've both been through enough together, and she's my best friend, so I think I get the most say in the decision."

"As I stated at the beginning of this mission, I'll

travel to the other holds and their cells, dispersing the leaks as best I can."

"And that leaves me," Thillan said, folding his arms across his chest and leaning back in his chair. "Well, I hate the Capital above all else, but I don't want to be far from my girl here. And since you're off on a grand adventure being our acting leader and all, I'll be the one to stay here as our cell's point of contact." Kamille smiled and nuzzled up against him.

"I'll be down to visit often, babe," she said.

"Then it's settled. Tomorrow, we'll get whatever gear we can manage and set out for the climb... Let's give the empire some Hell," Asher said with a clenched fist. Ayela smiled, feeling the spirit of their comradery, but eventually stared out the window through the blinders. Her thoughts drifted to Kacyn, Rhaja, Gean, and all those she lost...

...How many more would have to die before the empire finally falls?

Chapter 29

Thillan walked them to the gate and said his good-byes, hugging each of them and kissing Kamille like it was the last time they would see each other. "Try not to be strangers, girls. With Asher gone on his trip, I'll be a little lonely down here."

Kamille kissed him once more. "I'll be back to see you before you know it... Alright, we have to go while it's still morning. I love you."

"I love you too," Thillan said, walking backwards onto the town road. He waved at them as the gates began to close.

Once they were shut, Ayela took a deep breath and gazed across the open plains. It was a sea of rolling hills covered in green grass and with tall forests over the distant horizon. Then, they turned around and faced the massive mesa with the walled city of Bavylune at its peak. The city was so high in altitude that the waters pouring from the sewers eventually dissipated into a mist before they came close to hitting the ground.

They could see airships of all kinds far above them flying in and out over its tall walls. She'd heard stories of the infamous imperial capital; a sprawling metropolis, the symbol of wealth and culture of the empire. Its infrastructure was organized in circles of wealth, with the poorest dwelling in the outer circles, and only the most influential and powerful of Enthedrill's citizens living closer to the center.

In the middle of the city was a tower taller than any ever built, named the Emperor's Tower. It was a massive construct where the Emperor himself lived, but also where the highest military officials conducted their business, as well as where the hall of congress was located. At its base were the imperial interrogators; vicious military officials that employed unorthodox tactics to enact the Emperor's will. They were the torturers, dogmatic traditionalists and loyal patriots that often kidnapped citizens when they were hunting for persons of interest, like divine logicians.

Rumors spread throughout the empire that a glowing construct of alien origin hovered above the tower. They called it a grammatoginon – relics made of pure energy left behind after an aethril 'judgement' of a town. Those judgments were different than the attacks the Kult made when they summoned an aethril: they were random attacks by wayward aethrils for no readily apparent reason. The grammatoginon were often in the shape of a strange symbol, were white in color, and had the glow of whatever aethril left them. From what she heard, though, the one above the tower was in the shape of an upside-down cross – or a sword. No one could truly tell which one it resembled the most. What confused her, though, was its color...

...Red didn't belong to any of the aethrils her religion professed.

She sighed, admiring the natural beauty of the mesa as it stretched on for meters and meters to either side. It blocked the horizon behind it, and they were still far from the bottom. "We have half-a-day's journey to the base, then we scale the cliffside. There are plenty of cliffs, edges, and caverns on the way that are too small for anyone up top to notice," Asher explained as they began their trek. "We need to watch for the Kuslav Hawks near the top. The larger caverns are their homes, and they will seize any opportunity for a snack like us."

"We have everything we need, correct?" Kamille asked.

"That we do," Ayela confirmed.

"We should be fine. The important thing to remember is to stop if we're tired. We can take as many breaks as we need to. We have pistols at our hips and extendable rifles packed away in our bags for any threats we run into. If we catch the attention of a hawk, though... It'll be better for you girls to hide deeper into its cavern. I'll hold it off for as long as I'm able."

"Asher-"

"Don't fight me on this one, Kamille. These are the dangers of traveling in and out of Bavylune by climbing. If this is our only option, it's our only option. And divine logic isn't even on the table. We can't risk any possibility of the empire finding us, or any possibility of entering Bavylune for anything other than residence will be thrown away. If we are careful and mindful, we'll make it without any complication. It's not often people go missing by hawks, nor is it common for anyone worrisome to camp in the lower caves."

They were silent on their journey, thinking and overthinking about everything they faced trying to break into this city. Deep in her heart, Ayela wished there was another way to accomplish their mission, but she knew there wasn't. No other city had national connections like Bavylune. No other city had funding poured into its news networks, nor did any other have the kind of influential power it did. The house of the empire served as a symbol of authority; if the source was Bavylune, one could believe it to be true.

And that was what they were hoping for.

The trust in their networks was what they were counting on to reach as many as they could. She reminded herself of that hope, and tucked it away in the deepest parts of her heart. As they opened up small talk, light banter, and shared stories on their journey to the Capital, she kept the memories of Kacyn, Rhaja, Gean, the congregant masters, the officers in the congregation, and the townsfolk in the back of her mind.

Their lives served as spark that would see her mission through to the end...

Chapter 30

The first day was spent reaching the mesa and scaling up a portion of it.

The second day nearly brought them to the top.

The third day saw them safely to the sewer spouts that spewed water into the open air. The city had a complex sewer system, reaching deep into the mesa for its sources, while dumping the rest into the open air like this one did. The reservoir that the city tapped into was a complex system that constantly refreshed itself from the rivers flowing through the empire. The waters dumped into the air from the top were filtered thoroughly so that nothing but water would follow its flow. Nothing would pose a danger to anything below. When the founders of the city planned its construction, they believed it offered the waters back into the atmosphere, and helped to stimulate the environment in safe ways.

No matter the reasoning, they certainly never

planned for the three of them to use it as an entrance to sneak into the city. They stood at the windy opening, watching as hawks soared in the open air, and as ships roared overhead. Behind them, into the dimly lit sewers, they could smell the gross mixtures of waste and death. The diseased ones and the ghouls lived in its depths, and posed such a threat that soldiers were required to accompany maintenance workers when they descended. The three of them pulled their rifles out and opened them up, making sure their only defense was available if they needed it. Ayela only ever heard rumors, but they were enough to horrify her imagination. She envisioned wild and terrifying creatures. Images of artists' sketches and blurry pictures on the internet certainly didn't help.

"We know the drill from here. Our eyes will adjust the further in we go. I have the directions we need to take memorized, and it should take us far enough into the city that we'll be close to the broadcasting station. It'll be evening when we emerge, so we need to be mindful of night patrols from the police... Never has our mantra been truer than in this moment," Asher said. The girls snickered.

"Let's get moving," Ayela urged.

And so they began their trek. Their rifles were trained and ready, and as the sounds of the rushing waters quieted the further in they journeyed, their senses began to heighten. There was no conversation, no sounds they themselves uttered save for their careful, quieted footsteps. In the dim lighting overhead, they could barely see anything, but their eyes quickly adjusted to the dark. Every sound that they didn't make startled them, and in the shadows their eyes played tricks, lending to the idea that they couldn't be trusted.

But they pressed on, despite their fears, despite their anxieties of the dark. Hours went by as they trekked. Or had it been the day already? The girls weren't sure, and Asher kept his directions to himself – understandably, of course. No one wanted to ask questions and draw attention to themselves from the horrors that dwelt there. With them being so far from the entrance, every sound was amplified. Every drop of water, every soft patter of their footsteps, every heavy breath one of them would take. They worried that one sound loud enough would attract one of the foul creatures of the Capital's sewers.

Then Ayela paused.

For a moment, she was sure she heard a fourth walking among them. The others stopped and waited for her while she carefully surveyed their surroundings, but she found nothing. She nodded at the others and they continued. They didn't make it too far before she stopped once more, this time certain she'd heard the footsteps of another.

She turned around, and in the shadows behind them, she saw the outline of a tall figure with abnormally long limbs. Instinctively, she and the others raised their rifles, and they watched in horror as a creature with translucent skin stepped into the dome of dim light offered by the dull lamp above. Talons decorated its slender hands, and its rotted mouth bore sharp teeth that clenched angrily at them. What was worse were the hollowed eye sockets, full of emptiness and unnatural, unsettling oddity that paralyzed the mind and body. Asher could only muster one word against such terrorizing imagery, muttered between forced breaths;

"R-Run!"

The ghoul shrieked in a strange, bone-chilling cry, and they turned and ran as fast as their feet could take them. Suddenly, the sewers were full of noise, and both ghouls and the diseased chased them with voracious hunger and longing. The shrieks filled their ears, and she wondered how anyone above didn't hear them.

"We're almost there!" Asher yelled.

She saw the ladder ahead, but she saw the creatures beyond it as well. "There's too many!" Ayela panicked. Then, like a heroine from legend, Kamille unleashed her rifle on the creatures with hellish fury. The sounds of their pained cries replaced their growls and screams, and with the same zeal Kamille displayed, the rest of them opened fire on the monsters.

"We need to start climbing!" Asher shouted. He quickly ushered the girls to the ladder while keeping the creatures at bay. They climbed as quickly as they could with Asher right beneath them. The creatures seemed to vanish when their own were being picked off by gunfire, but they didn't trust their momentary peace.

Kamille was quick to open the sewer, not checking to see if they were in a street or alley. Ayela was the next to pull herself up and out. As Asher neared the top, though, one final creature tall enough to strike at him came charging from deep within the tunnels. Its monstrous shrieking filled the evening air with nightmare fuel, urging him to hasten himself as he climbed. He skipped ladder rungs as he rushed, and just as it seemed like it was going to be too late, the girls grabbed his arms and pulled him out just in time. The creatures talons swiped across the ceiling above it, knocking the ladder off its hinges as it screamed. They were quick to replace the manhole cover, sealing it in its dark and decrepit home.

The sighed in relief and rested for a moment, surprised that not a single sound could be heard from beneath them save for an occasional thud, presumably where the creature hit the ceiling. "I see that's how they fixed their soundproofing issue," Asher said in between breaths. The girls laughed.

"It's a relief to know they didn't hear any gunfire," Ayela added.

"That's certain enough."

"Ladies," Asher said, slowly rising to his feet. "Welcome to the Capital of the empire... Welcome to Bavylune." Ayela stood to her feet and looked around. The alley was in between two black-bricked buildings, sleek and clean in their design. The streets looked clean, though the alley was filled with debris and bags of trash piled around a big dumpster. Above them were clear, starry skies filled with passing hovercars. Her heart pounded in her throat and a grin crept across her face. All their effort culminated into that single moment, and a blissful realization came to mind...

...They finally made it to Bavylune.

IX

Episode 9

Revelations

Chapter 31

There she was, suspended in an empty void. Ayela. Was she Ayela? At this point, she couldn't tell. Her body seemed normal, but her hair was brown. Her skin was a little more sun-kissed. She gently placed her hands on her legs, her stomach, her chest, and then her ears. She paused at her ears.

Round tips.

Abnormal.

Smaller.

She was smaller than her elvish form that she was so familiar with. Around her was total darkness, like the expanse of space but without any stars. She looked around, her hair and clothes flowing as if she were suspended in water, but she could breath.

Her heart pounded faster and faster, as if there was a predator coming for her, but she saw no one. It didn't matter. She could feel their presence nearby. She frantically looked everywhere until her eyes rested on a ghastly spectral that forced the blood to drain from her face.

Fear.

She felt fear and terror, and tried to run, but she was on no surface to propel herself from. So she floated, frantically trying to jump, run, swim – anything to get away from the terrible image she saw before her.

Slender, skeletal fingers and limbs.

Covered head-to-toe in a thin veil.

Floating as she was.

She wasn't familiar with the darker gods of Rök's creation as some like the Towlålites were, but she knew enough to recognized Death when she saw it. And Death it was. The god of lifelessness. Aethril of void, emptiness, and nothingness. A dark servant of Rök that had only one purpose it craved; to cause the living to die. To ferry spirits. And what a perfectly easy job it had with the reman species; bodies without spirits. Or were they truly? Where was she now? This felt different than a dream. Here, she wore an astral form different than her elvish body, and yet similar.

"What do you want with me, Death?" She called out. Her voice sounded as though she were speaking across a great chasm.

"What do you want with me?" It asked in return, with a voice as ghastly and unnatural as its form. "Why do you pester my twisted shape, why do you seek to avert me from those of your kind?"

"Their lives are the only ones they get!" She retorted. Suddenly, her feet landed on solid ground, and her hair

and clothes rested on her as though gravity were sud-
denly returned. And then it answered her with a single
question that would stay in her waking memories...

"...Are you certain?"

She woke from her dream with a gasp in the dead
of night, dripping with sweat. Kamille had taken
one room, while Asher had taken the other. She laid
on her pullout mattress in the couch in her living
room. They'd been in the empire for three weeks
now, letting things settle after their excitement
in the sewers. The news reported the bodies of
the creatures after maintenance had to repair the
broken ladder, and that they found the empty shells
of their rifles. There were hunts going around for
any who were suspected to have been carrying high-
powered automatic rifles.

No one suspected them, though. Asher had
saved up enough sigil to hand her what she needed
to afford an apartment, and Kamille crafted the
perfect alibi to explain why their transit records
weren't showing up. Everything went off without
an issue, and she was able to take a job with a dance
school where she served as an instructor. They
settled nicely into the city and into its way of life.

Things were moving along as they all expected it to... Well, except for two things; her dreams, and the guy she was about to send a text to. His name was Kieran, and they met a week after moving into the city at a bar not too far from her apartment. Her chest was warm with excitement, and her mind was buzzing, despite her nightmare.

She thought he was cute, and though he hid his emotions, he was kind to her. She fantasized about him, envisioning his broad shoulders and blonde hair. He was toned, definitely easy on the eyes, but there was another important factor that kept drawing her attention to him – he was almost identical to the man in her dreams so many years ago.

Sure, his name wasn't Jack, he wasn't from some place called 'San Francisco,' nor did he have a friend named Elizabeth. But he looked so eerily similar, there had to be a connection. She kept the dreams about Jack to herself, though, and Kamille didn't trust him - and not just because he was an ivory elf. There was something about the aura around him that she didn't trust. Ayela herself was apprehensive as well, but she let him have his chance.

Hey. She wrote. His response was quick.

Hey, Ayela. I'm surprised you're awake right now. Everything okay?

Yea. I just had a nightmare, that's all. It was really vivid and weird.

Yea? What about?

She didn't know how to respond without sounding crazy.

It was weird, you'll probably think I'm weird.

Try me.

...It was about the afterlife. I saw Death, the korist god of nothingness...And it told me there was an afterlife for remans.

His response took longer than normal. She started to worry that she scared him off. Then he calmed her nerves.

That's pretty deep. How do we know, after all, that there's nothing after this? Has anyone come back from the dead?

Rhaja was the only one. She remembered that day like it was yesterday.

You're right. No one really knows.

Want to talk more about it over coffee tomorrow morning?

She paused, unsure of the right response. As she dwelt on it, though, she figured that she would be in the city for a long time, longer than Kamille. Why shouldn't she be allowed to open up romantically? Their mission wasn't for another week, anyways, so she had plenty of time to go on a date or two.

Sure! She wrote back.

It's a date, then. I'll pick you up at 8 so you have time to get to the school. You don't start until 9, right?

9:30, but I try to get there by 9.

I'll see you at 8, then.

See you then!

She sighed and set her phone down beside her, and with her fears and anxieties quelled, she drifted into more pleasant dreams...

...Dreams of a peace, romance, and happiness.

Chapter 32

A week passed.

The day was upon them.

The culmination of all their efforts. The sacrifice of Kacyn and the townsfolk. The memories of the congregant leaders that sparked their actions, and the data vaults with the secrets of the empire. Everything resulted in that day. It was the sum of their efforts. She woke early on that Saadas morning, and felt the weight of the mission at hand.

Ayela took a deep breath as she zipped up her black hoodie. She wore a pink tank-top underneath, and black jeans with casual sneakers. It was enough for her to blend in without notice. She tied her hair into a bun behind her head, made sure her makeup was minimal, and sighed as she looked herself over in the mirror. The others were ready for her to go, waiting on the couch for her to finish getting ready. She inhaled deeply, and roiled all her anxious tension in a long exhale as she emerged.

"Our shining star," Asher said with a smirk.

"That bloody boy-toy of yours should feel lucky he gets to be close with the one who's going to liberate his empire," Kamille said. Ayela rolled her eyes.

"He's got nothing to do with any of this. Besides, we aren't dating yet. We're just friends," she defended.

"Yet."

"Shove off, Asher."

"Alright, alright. We're just having a little fun. Kamille's the only one who doesn't really approve. I'm indifferent... You ready, Ayela?"

She nodded and smiled. "Yeah."

Kamille returned her smile and pulled her in for a hug. "You've got this, love. Don't worry. Once the secrets are out, the empire won't know what to do with themselves."

"Except maybe go to war with yet a third party."

"And we will be ready for that war, Ayela. Kamille will be here with you. Your divine logic will protect you. Whatever gods you believe in will come to your aid, as they've always done with your people."

Kamille rolled her eyes. "Gods or no, our goal is the same as it always was; to weaken the empire enough for something better to take its place...

"...Now let's go make that happen."

Chapter 33

She carried her thumb drive in her jacket pocket, nervously twirling it between her fingers. The streets were busy, full of residents and visitors alike. She could pick out the normal residents like with superior ease. They were all dressed similar; girls wearing tight leggings or jeans with white or grey jackets that hugged their figures, while the boys wore Henley shirts and harem pants with sandals to match. Visitors wore styles that represented their holds or towns.

She blended in seamlessly, even with her hood up. She kept her violet eyes from gawking at any one person for too long, and admired the towering buildings that reached for the heavens. All of them were pieces of art, and were either white or silver with golden trimming around their edges. Airships and personal hovercars zoomed through, treating the buildings like a maze where their greatest efforts were spent not crashing into each other.

The Emperor's tower was as terrifyingly magnificent as she expected, and as the rumors suggested, a red grammatoginon hovered over top of it in the confusing shape of an upside-down cross. Several enclosed suspension bridges protruded from different points all over the tower and extended to several smaller towers throughout the massive city. Near the tip, there were plenty of airships docked, and others that were leaving. It was a beacon of imperial pride, a symbol of power against all other odds that rose against it. And it once housed noble Emperors of ages long past.

Emperors that reigned in peace and humility.

She continued weaving through the crowds, focusing on her objectives despite the noise and overwhelming sensation of people bumping into her and shoving her aside. Everyone was busy, focused, energized. Everyone was so enthralled with their jobs and their agendas that no one could stop and appreciate the beauty of their own city.

Every so often, she would catch a conversation of someone on the phone, or between a loving couple about how much they enjoyed living in Bavylune and how exciting everything was, but most people were frowning automatons doing their best to make it through the day so they could go home and be tired and complain about being tired.

Was this truly how life was supposed to be for those who weren't affected by the Emperor's oppressive and restrictive laws? Was this the price of wealth and comfort? To be stuck in a time-consuming job that they hated, never growing and never moving, never enjoying the world they were put on? Were they just supposed to spend their youth wasting away at pointless jobs that only accomplish to keep a political and economic machine moving in aimless directions?

As thrilling as the city was, she hated it. She hated it as much as she hated Vör, the upper city of D'Vnora, the inner city of Ih'Dejj – she hated it all. Wealth and prosperity seemed to demand too much of a person for such a meaningless reward, and yet, there they all were struggling with all their might to acquire it. It was disheartening for Ayela to see.

She looked up, pulling herself from her own thoughts, and saw the massive satellite dish atop the square-shaped building. She arrived at the station in due time, and everything kept going according to plan. It would have to be the same as before; she needed to be invisible to the naked eye and cameras throughout. It would be easier this time now that she wasn't infiltrating a government facility. There would be more noise, more distraction, more opportunities for her to slip in unnoticed.

As she approached the entrance, just before she emerged from the crowd that surrounded her, she let her twisting fingers be the motion that kept her power flowing. No one noticed that she suddenly vanished out of thin air, nor did anyone notice that she shoved her way through and onto the streets. She moved quickly, dividing her focus as cars sped towards something they couldn't see. She dodged each vehicle just in time, careful not to break the motion of her fingers as she fumbled the thumb drive around in her pocket.

She made it safely across, taking the time to quiet her breathing before wedging through another crowd and onto the wide stairway leading up to the entrance. She waited for someone to open the door and quietly slipped in behind them, then repeated the process for every one she needed to get through. Asher went over the layout of the facility over and over with her before she embarked on this mission, so she was very familiar with its layout and where she needed to go to upload the video they made.

People were too oblivious to notice the slight gust of wind that hit them as she passed by in the halls, or the slight *pat pat* of her feet walking on the carpeted floors. She was careful, as careful as she could possibly manage. She let each person open each door and made sure their closure look as natural as possible. It was funny how easily she was able to slip by them.

Then she came to their newsroom, where the current show was airing. Patiently, she waited outside and watched, maintaining her invisibility as long as she needed. In what felt like hours, someone finally came to open the door during their break. Crews were busy cleaning the set and resetting what needed to be reset, and the media team quickly left for coffee. Some opened the door she waited at, offering her the perfect opportunity.

She snuck in and moved quickly while no one was around to notice and made her way to the first computer screen displaying the commercials. Everything hinged on that single moment. She inserted the drive and quickly pulled up the video that displayed the data on the imperial invasion.

Her senses were heightened as she flipped the switch, putting what her screen displayed on air. She let Asher's augmented voice explain the empire's hidden plot to control the people, and then pulled the thumbdrive out and walked away from the console. She hadn't felt as satisfied in her entire life as she did in that moment. Though no one could see it as they scrambled back into the room, she had a cocky half-grin.

It was too late. The signal couldn't be stopped in time. Already, too much had leaked, and a bug was programmed into the video that kept it on air and uploaded to the internet. The public knew who was behind the attacks on their own people, and they knew that the war on Durinveii was planned from the beginning. As she made her escape, her mind buzzed with their victory, knowing that she hit the ones who hurt her in such a way that they couldn't recover from. Not easily, at least.

Eventually, she made her way out of the station and back into the streets, and as she lost herself in the crowds, she reappeared to everyone's vision. Thankful that no one noticed, she pulled her hood back and let her hair down. She couldn't wipe her grin away, nor could she ignore the feeling she had deep in her heart...

...For once, the empire suffered instead of her.

Chapter 34

"It was all over the news," Asher exclaimed with the widest of grins. "Articles immediately published online, other news outlets tuned in to cover what happened, and the government scrambled to interview every single employee there. You did a good damn job, Ayela. We all did... I hope this serves as an appropriate revenge for the deaths of Kacyn, the congregation masters, and everyone else who lost their lives when this journey started."

She took a deep breath as she sat down beside Kamille. "...It's something. It's a blow to Emperor Gorvon's regime. It's an answer for the lives they tossed aside. That's all I need to feel some peace," she explained. She looked around at her apartment, and realized just how far she'd come in their journey. She had a home next to the seat of the emperor. She was an enemy, a threat to him, and he had no clue just how close she was.

"This is the end we wanted," Kamille said. "This is the victory we fought for. We fought a god, a cult, and monsters to get to this point. And here we are. This end needs to be a beginning, though. The darklings will know that we brought this victory, and they'll be ready for what you have for the Asher."

"You're right," he said, folding his arms across his chest. "So let's make this our battle cry. Tonight I leave for Shustur. I'll start there. I bought tickets for a shuttle tomorrow morning. After that, You'll be in charge of this cell here in the Capital, Kamille. It's only fitting that you head this one up, seniority and all... As for you, Ayela... Watch out for that boyfriend of yours."

"Hey-"

"I'm only joking!" He said with a sly grin, throwing his hands up. "...I'm going to miss you guys. This has been our best mission yet."

The girls let out a long *"aww"* and hugged him. "You'll be missed to..." Ayela said. "Be safe out there."

"...Always. Let's go get some drinks at that pub down the street and celebrate," Asher urged. They quickly grabbed their things and made their way to the door, but Ayela stopped to look back at her apartment one more time. Good things were coming for them, she could feel it. As they left, her mind lingered on one passioned question she longed to ask the spirit of Kacyn...

...Are you at peace now?

...Yes, Majjai...

I'm at peace.

Pronunciation Guide

Sümol [Sew-mall]
Ayela [Eye-la]
Rhexa [Wreck-suh]
Kamille [Kah-meal]
Karinth [Care-inth]
Lameen [La-mean]
Zadism [Zah-dism]
Korism [Core-ism]
Rök [Rook]
Skyrn [Ski-earn]
Salom'Sileyu [Sal-ohm-Sill-eh-yu]
Thaerv [They-erv]
Aethril [Eh-thrill]
Enthedrill [En-the-drill]
Songriveii [Song-rih-vey]
Durinveii [Dure-in-vey]
Songrivan [Song-rih-van]
Durinvan [Dure-in-van]
Daethril [Day-thrill]
Reman [Reh-man]

Uri'Kai [Yu-rih-kai]

Yglsora [Yi-gal-soar-uh]

Zachanel [Zah-shuh-nel]

Aethyrians [Eh-theer-ians]

Khebreh [Keh-Breh]

Khebric [Keh-brick]

Towlål [Tow-lawl]

Towlåalites [Tow-lawl-ites]

Korok [Core-Rock]

Dominov [Dohm-ih-nohv]

Vör [Voo-or]

D'Vnora [Div-nora]

Metralonia [Metruh-lonia]

Thallia [Thah-lia]

Bavylune [Bah-vih-lune]

Shamol [Shuh-mole]

Rhaja [Rah-juh]

Ethaynia [Eth-ae-nia]

Therapod [There-uh-pod]

Hashem [Ha-shem]

Laht'Med [La'T-med]

Tanbit [Tan-bit]

Gean [Gee-an]

Kudaj [Coo-dahj]

Numira [New-me-ruh]

Ynsigna [Yin-sig-nuh]

Kacyn [Kay-sin]

Ih'Dejj [E-Dej]

Bavylune [Bah-vih-loon]
Shustur [Shoo-stir]

X

Cast

A little bit about the cast of characters in this curious tale.

Orphaned Dancer

Character Details
Name: Ayela Rhexa

Sex: Female
Gender: Female
Sexuality: Bisexual
Age: 26 years (Thaervan timescale)
Species: Reman
Race: Songrivan Elf
Divine Logician: <u>Y</u>/N
Divine Logician Classification: Space-Time/"Dancer"
Place of Birth: Songriveii - Centerton [Assumed]

Talents: Martial arts (various schools), dancing (various schools), art, music (vocal), mathematics

Hobbies: Reading, writing, singing, art, dancing, hiking, movies, concerts, plays, cooking

Personality: Ayela is an emotionally driven person, but her intellectual prowess hides behind those emotions. She tries to see the best in people, despite having faced prejudice for her Songrivan ethnicity. She can be trusting to the point of naivety, and can sometimes be compromised by her emotions when making decisions. She is religiously devout, and can at times be aloof and absent-minded.

Summary: Ayela Rhexa was presumably born in Centerton, Songriveii, and was given up for adoption by unknown parents. She was left at the doorstep of an orphanage in nothern Enthedrill. Her name was given to her by the orphanage house-keeper, Kazitza Rhexa. She discovered her powers at a young age, and shortly found that she could control them with physical movements. She set out to learn various forms of dancing from several cultures, primarily her own (Songrivan), as well as various forms of martial arts. At the age of 16, her legal adulthood, she earned her citizenship after growing up with no one who wanted to adopt her. She spent her years honing her talents, keeping them a secret from all but a select few.

Her life was mostly a quite one until she met and formed a romantic relationship with her first partner, an ivory elf named Gean. The two were romantically involved for about a year before his life was claimed in an aethril attack. About a year later, she met her second romantic partner, a Durinveii native and gifted scholar named Rhaja. The two were romantically involved for about two years, and then her life was claimed in another aethril attack engineered by the elusive Kult of Salom'Sileyu. Her discovery and conflict with the Kult led to her eventual recruitment into the darklings.

The Spirit of the Witness

Character Details
Name: Rhaja Ethaynia

Sex: Female
Gender: Female
Sexuality: Lesbian
Age: 26 years [ATD] (Thaervan timescale) – Deceased
Species: Reman
Race: Durinvan Elf/"Dwarf"
Divine Logician: Y/<u>N</u>
Divine Logician Classification: N/A
Place of Birth: Durinveii - Leganum

Talents: Physics, mathematics, cultural studies, religious studies, art, astronomy, social science, language studies, computer programming

Hobbies: Art, stargazing, gaming (light), concerts, plays, hiking, reading, movies, shopping

Personality: Rhaja is intelligent, closed off, and can be considered cold by those who don't know her. She is often regarded as monotoned and mono-expressioned. She is academic and highly scientific, but lacks emotional intelligence. She's often curt and careless when it comes to the feelings of others, and doesn't show her own emotions to anyone except for those she's shown strong connections with, namely her girlfriend while she was alive, Ayela.

Summary: Rhaja was the daughter of a prominent Zadist family with political power in the country of Durinveii. She was a child prodigy who excelled at all academic subjects and was adaptive in learning new talents and abilities. She applied herself to her studies, and had a promising career in one of Enthedrill's top universities. Her superior intellect lended to her academic and scientific prowess, giving her a reputation as a gifted mathematician and astro-phycisist.

She was never truly religious in practice, but gave the possibility of supernatural beings some considerable thought. She embraced the spiritual concepts of Korism, despite her parent's protest. Also to their dismay, she embraced her queer sexuality as a matter of logic. Eventually, they learned to embrace it as well.

Later in life, she met Ayela Rhexa, a gifted dancer and Korist attending an Enthedrillan congregation that she also attended. The two became fast friends, and when she discovered she had feelings for the Songrivan, those feelings were reciprocated and they formed a romantic relationship. It would last a little over two years before Rhaja met her untimely demise at the hands of an aethril - a god of Korism, Zadism, and Kehbreh - controlled by Tallie, the master witch of the Kult of Salom'Sileyu.

Rhaja experienced an afterlife where she encountered the creator of all things, and eventually reincarnated as a human of unknown name after returning to thaerv in ethereal form to aid her still-living lover, Ayela. She continues to be a constant thought and memory for Ayela, though she is no longer present in any spiritual form, and is no longer in any sort of contact with her.

Mother of the Tribes

Kacyn

Character Details
Name: Kacyn (surname unknown)

Sex: Female
Gender: Female
Sexuality: Straight
Age: 21 years (Thaervan timescale)
Species: Reman
Race: Ebony Elf
Divine Logician: <u>Y</u>/N
Divine Logician Classification: Vision/"Farseer"
Place of Birth: Songriveii - Northton

Talents: Writing, poetry, story-telling, religious studies, baking, cooking, thievery

Hobbies: Reading, writing, star gazing, cooking, movies

Personality: Kacyn is gentle, tender-hearted, and perceptive. She is an empath by its very definition, and doesn't struggle with trying to understand what she can't understand. She is a woman of faith, and while she understands that violence is a byproduct of society, she still strives to achieve a more peaceful and loving world. She is docile by nature, shy, and tries her best to stay out of the public eye.

Summary: Kacyn was one of the many children kidnapped all over the world after displaying signs of divine logic. It was an initiative of the Kult to capture and indoctrinate children via cruel and abusive techniques so that they would aid in the dark endeavors of the Towlål. Kacyn was one of the few that resisted their efforts, and retained her pure heart and mind. She eventually escaped, and they struggled to recapture her (it was only after she united with Ayela, who Tallie attempted to keep track of, albeit unsuccessfully, that they were able to find her).

Kacyn suffered brutal torture at the hands of the Kult, and while there were no scars on her face, her clothing hid what scars she did have. She came to have faith in many gods, including the Towlål - several of whom were a subject of her active worship - but her primary focus in prayer, meditation, and worship was Rök, the high god of Korism. Her divine logic only draws her closer to her combination of spiritual beliefs. She believed that Rök was the one who spoke to her and helped her escape the Kult in search of Ayela, and she pulled together every resource she could to find her.

The Witch of Enthedrill

Tallie

<u>Character Details</u>
  Name: Tallie (surname unknown)

Sex: Female
Gender: Female
Sexuality: Lesbian
Age: 24 years (Thaervan timescale)
Species: Reman
Race: Ivory Elf
Divine Logician: Y/N (?)
Divine Logician Classification: Unknown. Tallie practices a foreign, unresearched magic.
Place of Birth: Enthedrill - Bavylune

Talents: Public speaking, espionage, poetry, gardening, language studies, martial arts (various schools), dancing (various schools), fencing, leadership, religious studies

Hobbies: Reading, writing, singing, dancing, concerts, plays, hiking, studying (history, religion, culture)

Personality: Tallie is manipulative and smooth, and she knows how to pretend to express concern and affection convincingly. She is incredibly intelligent, and knows how to hide her true intentions by displaying false emotions and luring people into a false sense of security. She lacks remorse, and only displayed any true emotion when the truth of her dark gods were revealed to her by Kacyn. Utterly, at her core, she does have emotions and feelings, but she has learned to effectively disassociate and disconnect from them to a detrimental and harmful extent. In the deepest recesses her heart, however, she never truly wanted to hurt anyone.

Summary: Tallie, whose lineage remains a mystery to everyone except for herself and her unknown parents, is the descendant of a long line of Warlocks that lead an organization called the Order of the Towlål, members of whom are called Towlålites. They renamed themselves "the Kult of Salom'Sileyu" in the modern era to disguise their organization from the public eye. Tallie remains an enigmatic, charismatic leader that holds deep-state power over many political officials in every nation, even the Sovereignty of Songriveii. Not much is known about her childhood, except that her parents were brutally strict and abusive when raising her. Their purpose was to extinguish any possibility of a kind-hearted woman, and ensure she would continue their dark work behind the scenes to bring about their ultimate goal; a universe totally claimed and reforged by their dark gods, the Towlål.

Under their tutelage, she learned deep and ancient magic that her order was famous for, and vowed to hone her craft until she could learn how do subdue and control gods. Her true goals and intentions remain a mystery, though. At times, she seems to have the goals of the Order in mind. At other times, she seems horrified at the idea of harming her fellow elves, but many have heard her mutter under her breath, "it's for the best," presumably giving towards the mindset that she's acting on what she believes is the greater good.

Hero from the Shadows

Character Details
Name: Thillan Orian

Sex: Male
Gender: Male
Sexuality: Straight
Age: 30 years (Thaervan timescale)
Species: Reman
Race: Korokian Elf
Divine Logician: Y/<u>N</u>
Divine Logician Classification: N/A
Place of Birth: Enthedrill - D'Vnora

Talents: Boxing, street fighting, creative writing, espionage, gaming, mathematics, social science, psychology

Hobbies: gaming, fighting, gardening, poetry, writing

Personality: Thillan is a quick-witted brawler with a knack for story-telling and gardening. He can come across as arrogant and self-absorbed, but inwardly he focuses on the people in his life and their well-being - almost to a detriment. He is a fighter, and channels his emotions - positive or negative - through fighting. When he's not fighting or gaming, he's usually seen with his girlfriend, Kamille. Hiding underneath his antics, however, lies a beaming intellect and a deep thinker that explores philosophical subjects, and while he typically surrenders leadership to someone he deems more capable, he thinks carefully before he makes decisions and weighs all options.

Summary: Thillan grew up in the D'Vnora under-city to lower class parents that relied on government assistance and housing. His parents did what they could to raise him as a kind-hearted man, but often times he would get himself into trouble. As a teenager, he joined a street gang that served as protectors for his district, wanting to give back to his community and protect them from rival gangs in other districts.

When he became an adult, his district was attacked by several elves posing as gang members, and his parents and many of his friends were killed when law enforcement stepped in. He suspected government involvement, and after pulling together his resources and everyone who was still alive in his gang, he infiltrated the local municipal and recorded officials discussing targeted districts to plant insurrection so that they could "control the population." After putting it on the internet and having those officials arrested, the darklings reached out to him and recruited him. Several years later, he met and began a relationship with Kamille Lameen.

Woman of the People

Kamille Lameen

<u>Character Details</u>
  Name: Kamille Lameen

Sex: Female
Gender: Female
Sexuality: Straight
Age: 28 years (Thaervan timescale)
Species: Reman
Race: Korokian Elf
Divine Logician: Y/<u>N</u>
Divine Logician Classification: N/A
Place of Birth: Enthedrill – Shustur

Talents: Kickboxing, computer programming, public speaking, espionage, gaming

Hobbies: Reading, movies, gaming, music (various instruments), concerts, public service, traveling

Personality: Kamille is emotionally closed off to most that she meets, but has an open, bubbly, warm persona when around those she considers friends. Despite her cold attitude towards certain races of elves, she truly cares for her species as a whole, and longs for a world where people aren't treated differently because of race and gender. She is an avid atheist, and trusts science and evidence above all else.

Summary: Kamille Lameen was the daughter of Nathim and Elsora Lameen, both of whom were immigrants from the Kingdom of Korok. She is one of two daughters, and was the first generation born in the Empire. Her parents were killed by law enforcement after they quarantined her city sector looking for a Songrivan refugee. Her sister was sexually assaulted as a child, and then subsequently killed, by an escaped convict days later. After the government seized any and all property and finances her parents left her, she was in foster care throughout her youth.

Ultimately, she ran away and left the public school system. She grew up with others like her, taught herself everything she missed out on from public learning, and was eventually recruited by the Darklings after defending an ivory elf, despite making her distrust and dislike of them clear. She was known for being an excellent hacker and exposed several prominent public figures for fraud, elicit activities, and bribery.

Darkling Mastermind

Character Details
Name: Asher Saya

Sex: Male
Gender: Male
Sexuality: Asexual/Bisexual
Age: 34 years (Thaervan timescale)
Species: Reman
Race: Ivory Elf
Divine Logician: Y/<u>N</u>
Divine Logician Classification: N/A
Place of Birth: Enthedrill - Ih'Dejj

Talents: Espionage, public speaking, computer programming, music (instrumentalist), piloting, professional driving

Hobbies: Reading, writing, poetry, hiking, movies, card games, exploring, skydiving, swimming

Personality: Asher is a smooth, silver-tongued leader that barely displays emotions, even to those he is closest with. He has a strong dislike and distrust of anyone who holds positions of power over the general public, especially the government. He is well educated and a man of class, and cleverly hides his association and leadership within the darklings from anyone that aren't in his immediate circle. He is extraordinarily intelligent, to the point where he unknowingly - and knowingly - treats almost all other people as inferior to himself.

Summary: Asher was born in a middle-class district of Ih'Dejj in the Empire. He often explored with his friends as a child, and would visit the kids of the poorer districts. One day, he saw one of his poorer friends die of starvation before he had a chance to get him any food. With overwhelming guilt over their death, he vowed to help the poor by taking food from his home and giving it to the kids who couldn't eat for that day. His parents, moved by his heart, helped him provide.

The empire stepped in an stopped him and his friends from continuing his efforts, and with the excuse of there being civil unrest and criminals hiding in that very same district, they opened fire on and killed many of the families that resided there. Asher spent his childhood, adolescence, and adulthood scarred from the empire's actions on his city and many of the other cities in the country.

He applied his learning throughout his teenage years to advanced computer skills and became an excellent hacker by his early twenties, and after exposing the actions of the governor of Ih'Dejj and getting him removed from office, he was approached by [Redacted] and helped to form the darklings. [Redacted] disguised themselves under the psuedo-name "Ruat," and he became a symbol of leadership and a voice for their mysterious leader. He became close friends with Thillan after personally recruiting him, and eventually became close friends with Kamille and Ayela as well. He holds in his heart a deep-seated hatred for the empire, and has vowed to see its institution torn down and replaced by a better government.

Deep-State Snow Elf

<u>Character Details</u>
  Name: Karinth Ignami

Sex: Male
Gender: Male
Sexuality: Asexual
Age: 38 years (Thaervan timescale)
Species: Reman
Race: Behemomnian Elf
Divine Logician: Y/<u>N</u>
Divine Logician Classification: N/A
Place of Birth: Behemomna - Nothenth Tribal Lands

Talents: Social work, espionage, exploration, piloting, computer science, mathematics, computer programming, political science

Hobbies: Reading, writing, poetry, hiking, exploring, skydiving, public service

Personality: Karinth is a gentle and caring snow elf that expresses strong empathy towards elves of all races. he is incredibly patient and is almost never seen angry. Despite this, he is also secretive, choosing only a select few to share deep knowledge and personal things with. While he enjoys interaction and being around people, he isn't as open as his personality might suggest.

Summary: Karinth was born on the northpole

continent of Behemomna, the ancestral homeland of the snow elves - the historical caretakers and guardians of the temple of the gods, which was considered a myth until recent discoveries. He was born to wealthy parents who raised him to be a caring and mentoring figure to the lost and hurting. As a child, he expressed great empathy for all forms of life, even plants.

When he grew into adulthood, he'd heard of the horrors of what the empire did to its citizens, and set out to immigrate to Enthedrill and help its people however he could. He attended a university in Shustur, and eventually became a social worker for Enthedrill's public services branch. For many years, he helped all people, and eventually caught the attention of the darklings. He refused to join, claiming that their methods were against his views that death - no matter how it was brought about - was a natural component of life. He did, however, agree to help them when they came to him, as a sort of information broker. This led him to his eventual meeting with Ayela in Vör.

At this point, he had proven to be a valuable asset to the empire, and convinced several officials to grant him top-secret clearance for some of the empire's greatest secrets. As he put it, this would let him aid the citizens of the empire in new ways. He, of course, would use this authority for personal study and to aid the darklings in their endeavors. What he was unaware of, however, was [Redacted] involvement in granting him that authority.

Prince of Songriveii

Character Details
  Name: Kudaj Renn

Sex: Male
Gender: Male
Sexuality: Straight
Age: 23 years (Thaervan timescale)
Species: Reman
Race: Songrivan Elf
Divine Logician: <u>Y</u>/N
Divine Logician Classification: Space-Time/"Dancer"
Place of Birth: Songriveii - Centerton

Talents: Leadership, Political science, religious studies, philosophical studies, martial arts (various schools), fencing, combat training, poetry, art

Hobbies: Poetry, art, physical training, martial arts training, hirstorical studies, cultural studies

Personality: Kudaj is fueled and driven by his anger towards the empire. He carries himself with maturity as the only surviving heir to the throne of the Sovereignty of Songriveii, but he also wears his emotions on his sleeve. He is calm when he's not on the battlefield, and loves to spend time with the people of his country that he believes he will one day inherit. He loves his family, his people, and his nation above all else, and expresses insatiable rage towards those who would threaten or harm any of that.

Summary: Kudaj is the second-born of Amadeus and Numira Renn, the Sovereign and Sovereigness of Songriveii. He comes from a long line of rulers and divine logicians through his mother, who is also his father's sister. He had a sister born three years before him, but she was kidnapped as an infant and presumably murdered. It was only later when evidence was found that implied imperial involvement in the theft of his sister's life, which sparked the war between Enthedrill and Songriveii.

He spent his childhood excelling academically and training as an elite martial artist. He expressed the signs of the space-time variant of divine logic at a young age, and channeled his incredible power through his martial arts. Growing up, he embraced strict discipline and practices, vowing to become a mighty warrior according to the prophecies of the court Farseer and his anger towards the empire.

In his adolescence and young adulthood, he became an accomplished soldier, expressing the desire to fight alongside his countrymen on the battlefield. He was known for being brutal against his enemies, but also for his compassion and love for his country and its people. He was loved and respected by his fellow Songrivans, and promised to be a just ruler in his sister's memory and honor.

In addition to his distinguished military and political prowess, he also formed a secret relationship with a Songrivan military commander named Jürdae Surr, a long-time friend of his on and off the battlefield. After the reclamation of Southton, he discovered he had true feelings for her, and would find a way to break his familial traditions to have a public romantic relationship with her.

Kudaj's Hidden Heart

Character Details
Name: Jürdae Surr

Sex: Female
Gender: Female
Sexuality: Straight
Age: 24 years (Thaervan timescale)
Species: Reman
Race: Songrivan Elf
Divine Logician: Y/N (?)
Divine Logician Classification: Unknown Classification
Place of Birth: Songriveii - Easton

Talents: Writing, poetry, music (instrumental), dancing (Songrivan school - Matriarch), martial arts (various schools), herbology, biology, psychology

Hobbies: Reading, writing, poetry, music (instrumental), movies, plays, hiking

Personality: Jürdae is a gentle spirit that enjoys nature, thought-provoking poetry and stories, and loves her country and people. She loves deep, meaningful conversation with close friends, but is relatively closed off and doesn't like to mingle in crowds too much. She's not outgoing, and isn't talkitive, but when she opens her heart to people, it can be overwhelming for someone who isn't as deep as she is.

Summary: Born to military parents Sasune and Naodia Surr, Jürdae was raised on the pride of her nation and its military, and formed a deep love and passion for her fellow countrymen. As soon as she reached adulthood at the age of 16, she joined the military with glowing recommendations from her parents and teachers at her school.

She climbed the ranks quickly, and attended Centerton's esteemed officer's academy at the same time as Kudaj, crowned prince of Songriveii. The two became close friends, and he often assigned missions for the two of them to go on together, stating that she was one of the few he trusted with his life.

With her military career and increasing prowess on the battlefield as an intelligent and tactical commander, she became valued by Songriveii's top generals, and earned Kudaj's attention and support. As they became closer friends, she grew feelings for the prince that were hidden until the night of the reclamation of Southton, where they expressed romantic interest in each other, albeit secretive due to the traditional nature of Songriveii's ruling family. He vowed to find a way to break the tradition and make their relationship a growing and public one.

Sovereign of Songriveii

Amadeus Renn

<u>Character Details</u>
  Name: Amadeus Renn

Sex: Male

Gender: Male

Sexuality: Straight

Age: 65 years (Thaervan timescale)

Species: Reman

Race: Songrivan Elf

Divine Logician: Y/<u>N</u>

Divine Logician Classification: N/A

Place of Birth: Songriveii - Centerton

Talents: Leadership, archeology, biology, international relations, cultural studies (exclusively Songrivan), music (instrumental and vocal), creative writing, cultural preservation, martial arts (various schools)

Hobbies: Poetry, reading, writing

Personality: Amadeus is a simple man, expressing only the base needs and wants a person could ask for. He values duty and loyalty above all else, but can also be merciful and forgiving to those who break their loyalty. He cherishes his family, and prizes tradition as sacred values in life. He carries the pride of his pure lineage, and bears the insult "blood elf" as a title of honor.

Summary: Amadeus is the son of Kalisada and

Agrago Renn, the brother - and husband - of Numira Renn, and successor to the long line of Renns who liberated Songriveii from the descendants of Majjai, the founder of Songriveii. This, of course, is subjective history based on its own texts, which are the primary texts that survived its long life as a country. No nation has lasted as long as the Sovereignty.

His parents began raising him and teaching him to be a ruler at a young age, and had him learn several schools of martial arts and creative writing. He became ruler of Songriveii at a young age due to his parents' untimely deaths, and married Numira as per the tradition of his family. For many years they tried to have a child, but they couldn't.

Eventually, though, Numira became pregnant with their first child, a daughter named Tsana Renn. Shortly after birth, though, Tsana was kidnapped by an unknown assailant, and was presumed dead when she was not found after a few years. Amadeus learned of imperial involvement in her kidnapping, and ignited a war with Enthedrill that persists to this day. 3 years after Tsana was born, Numira gave birth to Kudaj, who would grow to be a powerful divine logician like his mother, as well as a fierce warrior like his father. They continued to try to have more children.

In private, Amadeus learned that Tsana was illegitimate. Numira had an affair with someone unknown, and that was how she became pregnant with her daughter. Because of his love for Numira, though, he promised to raise her as though she were his own - until her eventual kidnapping and presumed murder. Kudaj remains *his* only legitimate heir.

Sovereigness of Songriveii

Numira Renn

Character Details
Name: Numira Renn

Sex: Female
Gender: Female
Sexuality: Bisexual
Age: 64 years (Thaervan timescale)
Species: Reman
Race: Songrivan Elf
Divine Logician: <u>Y</u>/N
Divine Logician Classification: Space-Time/"Dancer"
Place of Birth: Songriveii - Centerton

Talents: Writing, poetry, gardening, home design, public relations, dancing (various schools), martial arts (various schools)

Hobbies: Reading, writing, meditation, dancing, plays, concerts, wine tasting

Personality: Numira is a compassionate and emotional woman that has a deep love for art in all its forms. She loves to dance and express her thoughts and feelings in whatever artistic avenue she can. As passionate as she can be, however, she also has a fiery temper that isn't easy to calm.

Summary: Numira as Amadeus' sister was a playful and supportive child while they were growing up. While he received strict treatment and discipline that forged him into the leader he grew to be, she received their love and affection, and was doted on by them as a cherished princess.

As his wife, she served as his supportive partner in everything, and a voice of reason when he was unreasonable. They didn't have a perfect relationship from her perspective, though. She spent much of her adolescence and young adulthood questioning their strange, unorthodox family tradition, and wanted to break free from it.

She met [Redacted] and developed a close, strong relationship with him in secret, and eventually the two had an affair unbeknownst to Amadeus. It continued for a year until she became pregnant with Tsana, and she came forward with the truth to her husband after suffering immense guilt for her actions. He forgave her and vowed to cherish and love her daughter as though she were his own. This, of course, would not last, as Tsana was subsequently kidnapped and presumably murdered by imperial operatives. That, of course, is the official report, and what Amadeus believes.

Lord-President of Durinveii

Solacian Iona

Character Details
    Name: Solacian Iona

Sex: Male
Gender: Male
Sexuality: Straight
Age: 68 years (Thaervan timescale)
Species: Reman
Race: Durinvan Elf/"Dwarf"
Divine Logician: Y/<u>N</u>
Divine Logician Classification: N/A
Place of Birth: Durinveii - New D'Vnora

Talents: Fencing, music (instrumental), public relations, international relations, gemology, archaeology, paleontology

Hobbies: Reading, gemology, shopping, hiking, socializing, plays, concerts

Personality: Solacian is a strong-willed, bold personality that is passionate about his people and his country. He carries the "Dwarven attitude" with him wherever he goes, and never backs away from a challenge or fight. He is a very fluid and emotionally driven individual, and relies heavily on the council of others before making his decisions. His people often regard him as the wisest leader they've ever had.

Summary: Solacian grew up in the slums of New

D'Vnora, a city-state that mirrors the Enthedrillan hold it was named after. He applied himself to his studies growing up, and worked hard at helping his community pick itself up out of poverty. His parents were average middle-class workers, and devout Zadists. He grew up inheriting their beliefs, and embraced Durinvan culture despite the rise of the capitalist society that had taken over his country.

His parents worked hard to get him into university, and he excelled in political science. After graduating, he ran for office as mayor of his district, and spent his term improving the quality of life for his citizens while reducing the taxes imposed on them. He carried the same attitude and fire with him with each new position he was voted into, and eventually he won the election for Lod-President of Durinveii, making history as the first candidate of a minority party to win in Durinveii's modern history.

Emperor of Enthedrill

<u>Character Details</u>
  Name: Gorvon Komin

Sex: Male
Gender: Male
Sexuality: Asexual
Age: 59 years (Thaervan timescale)
Species: Reman
Race: Ivory Elf
Divine Logician: Y/N (?)
Divine Logician Classification: Unknown Classification
Place of Birth: Enthedrill - Bavylune

Talents: Public speaking, influence, historical research, cultural studies, religious studies, international relations, public relations

Hobbies: Baking, meditation, plays, concerts, woodcarving, fencing, martial arts (various schools), dancing (various schools)

Personality: Gorvon is silver-tongued, smooth, and cool. He's a charismatic leader that appeals to fascist and capitalist ideals. He believes in hard work, but also appreciates the finer pleasures in life. He respects and appreciates culture and religion, though he himself doesn't express and particular spiritual belief.

Summary: [Redacted]

About the Author

Zachael is a writer with a love for fantasy, science, and the allure of religious myth and cosmic theories.

You can connect with me on:
- https://www.zachaeltjp.com
- https://www.twitter.com/JZachael
- https://www.facebook.com/zachaeltjpresgrove
- https://www.instagram.com/zachael.the.writer